T·H·E
HAUNTING of Derek Stone

THE RED HOUSE
and
THE GHOST ROAD

TONY ABBOTT

APPLE PAPERBACKS

SCHOLASTIC INC.

NEW YORK   TORONTO   LONDON   AUCKLAND
MEXICO CITY   NEW DELHI   HONG KONG   SYDNEY

The Haunting of Derek Stone #3: The Red House
ISBN 0-545-03431-0, copyright © 2009 by Robert T. Abbott.

The Haunting of Derek Stone #4: The Ghost Road
ISBN 0-545-03432-9, copyright © 2009 by Robert T. Abbott.

These books were originally published by Apple Paperbacks.

ISBN-13: 978-0-545-20904-5
ISBN-10: 0-545-20904-8

12 11 10 9 8 7 6 5 4 3 2 1   9 10 11 12 13 14/0
40
Printed in the U.S.A.
First compilation printing, September 2009

THE RED HOUSE

To Those Who Cannot Leave

⊰| ONE |⊱

Mystery Boy

He *died.*

Two words, and my dumb little life changed forever.

Six letters, and the world I believed in vanished into nothing, like fog in the wind.

"I won't believe it!" I cried, falling to my knees. "I won't!"

"You must believe it," was the stone-cold reply.

As sunny and warm as the day began, night dropped hard and fast like the lid of a coffin.

The horror of it made me sick. I didn't want to go on. I couldn't go on.

I mean, how would you feel if someone told you —

Wait.

You couldn't possibly know how you'd feel unless you understood — really understood — what I'm talking about.

So let me wipe the blood from my forehead and go back nine hours to this morning.

I'll tell you everything that happened from that moment to now. You need to know where we came from to understand where we are now.

We? Right. Let me start there.

My name is Derek Stone. I'm fourteen, fat, smarter than most people I know, and on the run. Nine hours ago, my older brother, Ronny, and I were holed up in a filthy room in a fleabag hotel on the outskirts of Baton Rouge, Louisiana. We'd been there since four a.m. the night before.

It was 11:21 a.m. when I opened my eyes. The blinds were down, but sunlight sliced through them like a hot knife through butter. The air was a white haze. The room was an oven.

"How'd you pick this dump, anyway?" I asked Ronny, rolling off the mattress and onto my feet. "I feel horrible."

"You look horrible," Ronny snorted from the bathroom sink. "Being on the run means being on a budget. Our money's almost out."

I flipped open my cell. Black screen. Dead battery. "I wish I could charge this thing," I said. "In case Abby calls again."

Abby Donner. My phone had died last night in the middle of a call from her.

More about her later.

"Toss that thing," said Ronny. "The cops can trace it, right? Besides, Abby's train comes in half an hour. Get dressed."

I pulled on my pants and shirt and muscled Ronny out of the bathroom. I held my breath as he passed.

Why did I hold my breath? Because Ronny is decaying.

"Decaying?" you say. "The dude's only nineteen. How could he be decaying? Only corpses do that, right?"

Right. Only corpses.

Man, I'm tired of telling this story. But you need to hear it. Your life depends on it, though you may not know it yet. So listen up, and bear with me. There's a lot to tell, and not much time.

A few weeks ago Ronny, my father, and I were in a bad train wreck. Maybe you heard about it. Big news. The old bridge over Bordelon Gap collapsed. Our train fell into the ravine. Ronny was one of nine passengers killed.

Then he came back.

Came back?

Trust me, that's the easy part.

"We're out of here," Ronny said. He pulled me into the hotel hallway with all my worldly possessions:

twenty-something dollars, twenty pounds of extra fat, a headache, and a case of the shakes.

"Let's skedaddle," he added.

Skedaddle? That's exactly what I'm talking about.

Ronny came back from the train wreck — at least, his body did. Inside him was the soul of a young man named Virgil Black. Virgil died in an almost identical train crash at the same place back in 1938. Because the two accidents were so alike, and because the curtain that separates the worlds of the living and the dead has been torn — I call it the Rift — souls in the afterlife were able to enter the crash victims at the moment they died.

"Enter the crash victims?" you say.

Yep. Reanimate them.

Like, "Hello! We're back!"

It's the old body, but a different soul. I call this grotesque process of soul-switching *translation*.

Another one of the train wreck victims was my father. He was missing for weeks, presumed dead, since all they could find of him was his hand. But then he turned up alive and *un*translated . . . I think.

The souls who came back at the crash site are a pack of notorious convicts, led by a murderous thug named Erskine Cane. I'd learned pretty quickly that these dark souls are only the advance troops of a massive dead-guy army called the Legion.

The Legion.

The word makes me nauseous.

"Come on," Ronny said, slinging his small bag into the trunk of a beat-up green Subaru that belonged to his ex-girlfriend, Samantha. It had looked much nicer before we'd borrowed it. "Clock's ticking."

I slid into the passenger seat.

According to Ronny — or Virgil — for centuries, the evil souls of the Legion have been warring against good souls in the afterlife. And they're winning. Once they discovered the Rift, they began translating into dead bodies and bringing their war up here.

Why?

To take over.

Since Virgil is a soldier on the good side, he knows that evil souls are angry, vindictive. They want revenge on the good, on the living, on everyone better off than them. Ronny told me that the afterlife of evil people is like perpetual torture. It's horrible. So the dark souls want out. They want to come back here.

No matter what it means for the living.

In addition to Cane, who returned in the body of a giant, muscle-bound soldier, there was a strong wiry dude with a nervous tic who I call Twitchy. Another convict returned in the body of the train conductor, who lost an arm in the accident. There's also an amazingly tough gray-haired old man. He beat me up once. I definitely don't like him.

There are three or four others, too.

Or there were, until last night.

Last night, the Legion picked up another fifty or so evil souls in a place called Bayou Malpierre. Those souls — in the bodies of bayou tourists — are led by a creepy little blind boy named Waldo Fouks. The soul inside Waldo's body is actually the leader of a murderous band of riverboat smugglers.

Nice, right?

Waldo was totally weird. But he did tell me I was "special." He called me "mystery boy."

I hope that goes in my permanent record.

"I don't like this," Ronny said. He slowed the car and pulled over to the curb to let four police cruisers tear past us.

"You don't think they know about us, do you?" I said.

"Maybe," he said quietly. "Maybe Uncle Carl told them to look for us." The police cars roared up the street and away. After a minute, Ronny pulled back into traffic.

My father's brother Carl had stayed with me in New Orleans after the train crash. He was there when Ronny came back, but he didn't know the whole story. He just thought Ronny was out of sorts, traumatized. He couldn't have imagined the truth. Uncle Carl was out of town when Erskine Cane burned down our house in the French Quarter.

Ronny and I had been hiding out ever since. It was only a matter of time before the cops got involved, really. With a mass translation in the bayou, with Dad leading the cops on a wild-goose chase so we could get away, with people "dying" and then mysteriously "coming back," the cops would soon be all over our war with the dead.

The war, I called it.

Simple but effective.

"I'll park a few blocks from the station, just to be safe," Ronny said. Then he snorted. "Safe? Some joke, huh?"

Neither one of us was laughing.

But it gets worse.

Over the last few days, I've learned that the Legion is searching for someone called the First — the first one translated. He's here, in the world of the living. From what I'm getting, the First is the Legion's ultimate leader here. He's even worse than giant Cane or creepy Waldo. Great.

Ronny paused at a light, searching right and left for a good parking spot. More police cars roared up behind us, lights flashing, but no sirens. Ronny grumbled and turned down a side street.

So how do I know about the First?

Because everyone keeps telling me, that's how.

To begin with, Abby Donner — the girl we were going to meet at the train station — was in a coma after the crash. She says that while she was in the coma, her mother, Madeline Donner, came to her and told her about the Legion. And Abby remembers it. What Abby doesn't know is that her mom's body is now inhabited by the soul of Erskine Cane's crazy wife. And, like Ronny, she's decaying, too. Pretty bad, huh?

I've seen Cane's wife a few times already, and each time she told me the same thing.

"The First . . . " she said. *"The First . . ."*

As if she was trying to warn me or something.

I guess it makes sense that anyone related to Abby wouldn't be all bad.

Oh. Something else happened in Bayou Malpierre, too. Ten years ago, when I was four, I nearly drowned there. I was under that murky gray water for a long time. And while I was almost drowning, I apparently *saw* the First. At least that's what my dad told me.

Of course, I have no memory of what really happened in the bayou ten years ago. But did that stop the dead from haunting me? Not so much.

You also have to know that Waldo Fouks's father, Bonton, was actually a decent guy, who died defending Ronny and me from his creepy son. He didn't know who Waldo really was until then. Just before he died, Bonton gave me a photograph of an old red house. He'd found it on me when I was little, after I was saved from drowning, and he kept it hidden for ten years. When I saw the picture again, I knew that house right away. I just didn't know how. Or why. Call me crazy, but I also knew that the rusty iron key I had found would open something in the red house.

Abby had called the night before to tell me that she had discovered the location of the mysterious red house. So Ronny and I hightailed it to Baton Rouge to meet her. We had to get to the red house — wherever it was — before the Legion did.

Time was running out. They'd left the bayou in search of the red house themselves, almost as if someone had commanded them to.

The First?

That's what I'm thinking. But what do I know?

All I knew for sure was that we had to find that red house, figure out what the key opened, and hope that it would help us stop the Legion before they took over the world.

Not much. Just that.

"Here we are." Ronny stopped the Subaru at a curb three and a half blocks from the train station. "Hurry it up, Tubs."

There's love for you. One of the weirdest things about Ronny is that even though he's Virgil Black now — a farm boy from upstate, in Shongaloo — there are still bits of Ronny in him. An occasional look. A phrase. A gesture. Something.

So I still call him Ronny.

Virgil doesn't seem to mind.

I followed him along the sidewalk. It was 11:51 a.m. Our day had begun.

◅| TWO |▻

Abby Donner

Abby's train was due at noon, and it was four minutes to twelve by the time we arrived in the main concourse of the train station.

I was about to tell Ronny how being anywhere near trains made me sick to my stomach, but then I saw the blazer.

Navy blue, shiny, saggy in the shoulders, with a bulge under the left arm. And then another blazer just like it, and another, and another. Between and above the baggy shoulders were thick necks, sweaty foreheads, and darting eyes.

"Police?" I said. "Federal agents?"

Ronny glanced furiously from face to face as the men moved quickly into every corner of the large room. "This is bad. If they bring us in, they won't believe a word we say, and the Legion will keep growing until it's too late. Slip into the shadows. If I lose you, I'll meet you on the street behind the building. Keep out of sight. We may have to start running."

Running? That loosened something in my head, and strange words echoed from my memory.

Children of light, lost, so lost, running in darkness . . .

I shivered to hear those words in my mind. Like other words I'd "heard" since the accident, I had no clue what these meant. But they sure seemed to be about Ronny and me.

. . . lost, so lost, running in darkness . . .

And maybe Abby, too.

Ronny pulled me out of the main room toward platform thirteen. We ducked into a bagel shop when a couple of guys in blazers passed.

"Uh-oh, Ronny," I whispered. "Look up there."

A flat-screen TV behind the counter showed grainy nighttime footage of water rushing through a big swamp.

Bayou Malpierre. I knew it.

My chest buzzed when a TV voice-over began describing the incident. I couldn't hear everything, but I could hear enough. "Flash flood . . . broken lock . . . crested levees . . . bayou tour boats . . . startling rescue . . ." The video then showed a car hidden among the bayou overgrowth.

Our green Subaru.

"That's it," Ronny said. "They know about the car, and they're closing in. There's her train."

The train from New Orleans squealed to a stop, and right away the platform was flooded with passengers. We waited in the bagel shop, scanning the crowd. Almost the last person to leave the train was a girl with long brown hair tied in a loose ponytail. Abby Donner. She wore blue shorts and a green T-shirt, and had a big handbag slung over her shoulder.

Abby had broken her ankle in the train wreck a month ago, but when she walked down the platform, I saw that her ankle cast was gone. She was using a wooden cane.

"I'm going," I said.

Ronny grabbed my arm. "Wait for her to come a little closer —"

"I'm going." I pushed out of the shop and walked quickly to the platform, head down, hoping no one would notice me.

Abby's eyes were tired, and her face looked pale, but she managed a smile when she spotted me. "Hey, Derek."

"We can't be here," I whispered, taking her arm.

"Hello to you, too," she said, stopping. "Do you even know how much guts it took for me to get on a train again, or what I went through to find that weird old house for you?"

"Do you even know how many cops are in the station right now, waiting to nab us?" I whispered.

Her face changed. Narrowing her eyes, she scanned the concourse. "Whoa. Okay, head for the west exit. It's closest. Believe me, I scoped it out. I had all kinds of maps and diagrams and I used MapQuest and —"

"Just come on," I said, and we hurried down the platform.

Some army, huh?

A fat boy, his dead brother, and a chatty girl with a cane.

We didn't stand a chance.

All at once, someone in a blue blazer bolted across the concourse toward our platform. A shrill whistle sounded, a man yelled, and agents fanned out across the big room. I glanced over at the bagel shop. Ronny was gone.

"Let's get out of here!" I hissed. Abby and I took the first set of stairs we saw.

"Just so you know, I don't like stairs," she said.

But there was no choice — she half-jumped down as quickly as she could. We made our way to street level and hurried down a tunnel, nearly colliding with Ronny, who joined us from a connecting tunnel.

Together, the three of us hustled through two or three more passages and out a service exit.

"Where's the car?" asked Abby, once we reached the sidewalk.

Before Ronny or I could answer, three police cars tore down the street toward the green Subaru.

"How about we walk?" I said.

"And let's make it fast," Ronny added, looking both ways and pushing through the gathering crowd to the curb.

We darted out into the street between lights and among cars. Horns blared. Drivers shouted. We didn't care.

More police cars raced down the street, but we were already gone.

◁| THREE |▷

The Memorial

We hustled through the hot streets on foot, first with Ronny in the lead, then Abby. I knew she was in pain, hobbling on her healing ankle, but she said nothing except "Right," "Left," and "Straight ahead."

"Where are you taking us?" Ronny panted.

"School," she said.

"What?"

But Abby just hurried on.

Ronny looked back over his shoulder constantly. The gray patch on his neck was bigger than I remembered from last night. Darker, too.

A half hour later, we huffed and puffed our way through the tall cast-iron gates of Louisiana State University.

"School, huh? Why are we here?" Ronny asked as we entered a broad avenue lined with poplar trees.

"The war memorial," Abby replied simply.

"Oh, yeah? Which war?" Ronny grumbled with a scowl. He didn't sound as if he really expected an answer.

We took several more twists and turns, and before long arrived at a structure that looked like a bank with a clock tower sprouting out of the top like a mission steeple.

"This war memorial was built to commemorate the Louisianans lost in the First World War," Abby said. "In the basement is what's left of something called the Dixie Museum. It has tons of documents and photographs and stuff relating to the Civil War in Louisiana."

"And?" said Ronny.

"And," Abby continued, "I'm pretty sure it's got information about your red house."

My heart thumped as I pulled the old photograph from my pocket. "Really, you found this place?"

"Sort of," she said. "You'll see. Come on."

Abby and I started up the memorial steps, but Ronny was frozen, staring at a little old car in the nearby parking lot. A student in a baseball cap had just gotten out of it and was now hustling past us, into the memorial.

I looked at Ronny. "What's the big deal?"

"He left his keys in the car," Ronny said quietly.

I snorted a laugh. "Who'd want to steal that thing, anyway?"

"Yeah, who?" Ronny snickered. Then he turned to follow Abby up the stairs and inside.

After passing the security checkpoint, we headed for a bank of elevators. Abby pressed the down button.

"Uh . . . I don't like being cooped up in iron boxes," Ronny mumbled, his eyes darting everywhere. "I'll take the stairs."

Ping! The doors opened. The elevator was empty.

"We'll meet you one floor down," Abby told Ronny.

"Yeah, yeah," he said. "I know where basements are."

He slunk off down a hallway, and the elevator doors closed on me and Abby.

"He's not doing so well, is he?" she asked, turning to face me.

I shook my head. Ronny's finger was black with rot where he had cut it trying to shave, and the tip was gone. The gray patch on his neck was getting bigger by the day. And those were just the places I could see. I knew the rotting smell made him avoid close quarters, like the elevator. It was an ugly thought, but I wondered how long Ronny would be around before he decayed completely.

Of course, the big question was why Ronny was decaying so quickly in the first place — even though the Legion wasn't. I had theories. It seemed to have something to do with *where* they died. Ronny died on the rocks in the ravine, on land. So did Madeline Donner, who also seemed to be decaying. But those who died in the water hadn't started to decay.

Not yet, at least.

Whoosh. The elevator doors slid open. It was cooler in the basement, and the air smelled like musty old paper.

When Ronny joined us, we walked through two rooms of the little museum before slowing in a third.

"I had almost nothing to go on," Abby said. "You have an old photograph of a red plantation house. My mother told me the dead are searching for a red house, too. But I knew there must be a thousand red houses in dozens of parishes all over the state. So, since your photo is so old, I went way back in the past."

"What did you find?" I asked.

Abby led me to a glass display case marked "Pre-War Plantations Lost and Found." She tapped the glass over one of the photographs there. "Is this it?"

I gasped.

It was the same house in the photograph that Bonton had given me. The angle was different, and the house had changed over the years, but I recognized it instantly. Its walls were tinged red, its roof sagged, two of the monumental columns were cracked and leaning, and the cast-iron fence that showed the same floral design as the iron key was flat on the ground.

Trembling, I focused on the typewritten label next to the photo as Abby read it aloud.

"The house is called Amaranthia — Derek!"

I slumped to the floor and blacked out for a second. When I came to, my head burned and my bad ear buzzed.

Ronny knelt next to me. "Could someone please get some water?"

A female security guard hurried over and helped me into a nearby chair. I sat with my head between my knees to get the blood flowing again.

"It must be the terrible heat," the woman said sympathetically.

It wasn't the heat.

"Amaranthia," I said softly. "Amaranthia."

And words I'd heard somewhere before came to me again.

Within your crimson walls, I was an angel child;

From room to room I floated in your wingless window light . . .

"The house is named after the amaranth flower," Abby said, patting my hand the way they do in old movies when you faint. "It's a big red blossom, almost coral."

I knew all that, of course. How I knew it, I couldn't say. Odd things had been sloshing around in my head ever since the accident — words, names, sounds, voices. And all in the ear in which I'd heard hardly anything since I nearly drowned ten years before.

Completely weird, I know.

"I'm okay," I said, standing and walking slowly back to the display.

Like tumblers falling into place, snippets of knowledge and fact, memories, maybe even dreams, all shuttled across the surface of my mind until they found their proper positions. Something clicked.

"Amaranthia was the ancestral home of the Longtemps family," I said. "My mother — our mother," I said to Ronny, "was a Longtemps. The house is a few miles from Compson, in Coushatta, on the Red River."

Ronny scowled at me. He was Virgil Black now, not Ronny Longtemps Stone.

"The Red River," he said. "What a surprise."

I knew what he meant. Every translation so far had been on or near the Red River or one of its tributaries. The Red River ran hard and fast through Bordelon Gap. Bayou Malpierre was on the Atchafalaya, an offshoot of the Red River. And now we were headed to Coushatta, on its banks.

How I knew where the house was — without even looking at the display — made no sense. A total mystery. But it wasn't the biggest mystery.

I had never been to anyplace called Coushatta. I doubted I'd ever even said the word out loud. But in my mind I saw its grassy green banks sweeping up from the river to a big lawn, and a garden dotted with wild amaranth blossoms as the morning sun hit them after a long rain.

What was that? A painting? A memory? What?

"Amaranthia was built in 1821," said Abby, reading from the exhibit. "It was a plantation at the center of a hundred-square-mile tract of land that spanned both sides of the river."

Leaning over the photograph, with my hands braced on the glass cabinet, I said, "I know all that."

"Why does that not surprise me?" said Abby. "Derek, you are —"

Her cell phone rang. Her face flushed when she saw who was calling. She raised the phone to her ear. "Hi . . . No, I'm fine. Nora, I'm absolutely fine. . . ."

Abby was talking to Grammy Nora, her grandmother, a cool lady who didn't quite believe what Ronny and I had told her about the living dead, but who loved her granddaughter and so had helped us.

"Because I can't get you involved in this . . ." Abby said.

I heard Nora practically screaming on the other end of the line.

"Did you skip out without telling her?" I whispered.

Abby gave me a look. I shut up. "Grammy, I love you. I know, but trust me. My mother came to me. She told me about the house. Trust me. This is important."

The voice on the other end began to speak more softly.

"I know," Abby went on. "And I will. Look, these guys are all right. They'll take care of me." She pulled the phone away from her face and whispered, "You'd *better* take care of me!" Then back in the phone: "I know. I will absolutely call you tonight. Baton Rouge. Right. I love you, too."

Listening made me sad. Sad for Nora, who didn't know the half of it. Sad for Abby, who would soon figure out her mother was one of the translated dead. Sad for Ronny, who was on the wrong side of being dead. And sure, I was sad for me, too. Why not? I was smack in the middle of this horror.

"The Longtempses were a powerful family, but the Civil War changed everything," Abby read from the display. "The family lost its land acre by acre. Only a few fields and the shell of the house remain today."

I didn't say, "I know" — but I did. I knew everything she said. What place in my mind held all this weird information? What kind of freak was I?

"Amaranthia was known as the 'Jewel of Coushatta,'" I said randomly.

"It's hours from here," Ronny added.

Did my mother know about her family's house? Was she the one who first told me about it so that I remembered it? I hadn't seen her for ten years. All I could recall was standing next to her in the cemetery before she left my life forever.

"The house is now derelict, inaccessible from modern roads," Abby read.

I pulled the old key from my pocket. It was rusted iron but not large, so I knew it wasn't a house or gate key. I instinctively knew it belonged to something in the house. The floral pattern inside the key's oval grip was the same amaranth as on the fence, the doors, everything. "Maybe it opens a chest, or a closet door," I murmured.

"Or a box or a desk drawer," said Abby.

"Okay, look," Ronny spat, pacing the room like a caged tiger. "First of all, keep your voices down. And second, the Legion saw you with the key in the bayou, Derek. They'll know about the house. We don't have time for guessing games. We have to find what the key opens, and we have to do it now."

"Maybe they don't know where the house is," Abby whispered.

"They know," said Ronny sharply, his eyes shooting around the room. He moved toward the door. "They aren't people, remember. They're the Legion. Centuries of warring in the afterlife have made them different from you and . . ."

Ronny trailed off. I knew why. He was about to say, "Different from you and me." But that wasn't true. He was like them. A dead soul, back again.

"Ronny, listen," I started, but a sharp, lemony smell wafted into the room and distracted me. I turned to Abby. "Are you wearing perfume?"

"What?" she asked.

Suddenly, the air thumped, and shards of wood and glass sprayed across the room. I was thrown to the floor. Alarms went off. Sprinklers spurted. Abby screamed. Ronny yelled.

Then came a second blast. More glass flying — and the sound of running feet.

◄ FOUR ►

Rest Stop

Was it seconds? Minutes? Longer? I couldn't tell you.

Sirens whooped in my good ear. Sprinklers spurted, and the water mixed with the dust in the air, muddying the floor. The security guard scrambled to her feet and called for help on her walkie-talkie. "Injuries . . . basement of the memorial . . . Hurry . . ."

I wondered for an instant if she was talking about me. But when I got up, I knew I wasn't hurt badly, even though I'd been thrown across the room. I hoped Abby was all right. I didn't see her anywhere. I knew Ronny would be okay — he'd been halfway out of the room at the time.

"Abby!" I called out.

Then I saw someone, half-visible in the smoke, rolling on the floor. I was afraid it was Abby, but just then Abby rushed toward me out of the dust, waving it from her face as two men in uniform burst into the room. The guard pointed her walkie-talkie at the student in the baseball cap, and they hurried across the room to him, ducking under the sprinklers. The student was clutching his leg and groaning loudly.

"Come on," said Ronny, appearing out of nowhere and grabbing my arm. "We need to go. Now."

We left the room in chaos. Ronny took us up the stairs. It was mayhem in the lobby, too. Everyone was being checked quickly, then evacuated, but we couldn't have that. What would they find if they checked Ronny? A troop of armed security and medical people raced past us. With all the distractions, we were able to sneak by the others and hurry to the parking lot, Abby hobbling quickly on her cane.

Ronny went straight to the little old car he'd spotted earlier. "Get in," he said, climbing into the driver's seat. "That guy won't be needing it anytime soon. We're doing him a favor."

"Wait a second, Ronny —" Abby started.

"Get in!" he commanded.

We did. He started the car. "Full tank. Good thing. We don't have money to spare on gas."

We pulled into the line of cars being rushed off campus.

"Why did that happen?" I asked after a minute. "Who did it?"

Ronny shook his head. "I don't know, but it wasn't much of an explosion."

"Oh, no?" Abby said from the backseat. "That guy looked pretty hurt —"

"I know he was hurt," Ronny said, "but from the glass in the display case. Not shrapnel. Not exploding metal. Not a real bomb. I know about those things. This wasn't the same. This wasn't the Legion."

I knew that Ronny was right. It wasn't the Legion. But it wasn't the explosion that made it clear. It was because there was no water. The Legion was always near water.

Abby and I glanced at each other. I knew we were both thinking the same thing. If not a big bomb, if not to hurt us, then who set it off and why? I remembered the smell of perfume just before the explosion. Why did I bother to notice it in the first place? Did it mean anything?

As more emergency vehicles flew past, Ronny finally tore out of the university campus and onto the street again, heading out of the city.

"There's something else I need to tell you," Abby said hesitantly. She closed her eyes for a second, then opened them. "My mother . . ."

Uh-oh, I thought. "Yeah?"

"She's dead . . . and not dead, isn't she?"

"What?"

I didn't know what to say.

"She's been translated. You're trying to keep it from me, but I'm not stupid. Just stubborn. She died in the train crash, but she's back, isn't she? It's the only thing that makes sense."

Abby waited for us to speak, but there was nothing to say.

She let out a deep breath. "There's more. The longer I'm out of my coma, the more I remember stuff my mother told me. I think I'm supposed to pass it along to you."

"To us?" said Ronny.

"No. I mean Derek," she said. "Last night I thought of a word, and it knocked around my head for a while until I finally said it out loud. But it was my mother's voice that I heard. It was a word she had told me when I was in my coma."

"What word?" I asked, not entirely sure I wanted to know.

"Messenger." Abby paused for a moment. "I think she said that she's some kind of messenger. From there."

"The afterlife?" said Ronny.

Abby nodded. "I mean, she knew about the red

house, even before you got the photo. She knew they're called the Legion. There's probably more, I'm not sure. But I think she's on the good side and she's telling me things you need to know, and so I have to stick close to you."

How was I supposed to deal with that?

"Uh, thanks?" I said, embarrassed.

"Oh, don't thank me!" she said with a quiet laugh. "I don't think I'm going to tell you anything good, but — Ronny, be careful! We want to make it to Coushatta, not crash halfway there!"

Ronny grunted and eased off the accelerator. I was used to his terrifying driving skills by now, but this was Abby's first taste.

"Fine," he said. "But Coushatta is in Red River Parish, two hundred miles from Baton Rouge. I have to stay off main roads because of the police, so you're going to have to sit tight for a few hours."

Sit tight? We had no choice. It was a subcompact.

Hour after hour went by. It was late afternoon, almost five, when we saw a sign for a town called New Compson.

"New Compson was mentioned in the museum display," said Abby. "Amaranthia isn't far away."

"I thought it was just called Compson," I muttered distractedly.

"Why do you say that?" asked Ronny.

I thought about it. "I don't know." That bothered me. It was like an encyclopedia had opened in my brain the instant I heard the name of the house, but there was way too much information, and I couldn't access it fast enough.

"Well, it should be just plain Compson," said Abby, gazing out the window. "There's nothing new about it. Look at those cars! It's like that vintage car museum I saw once with my . . . my . . ."

She didn't finish.

But she was right. The town's main street was scattered with cars and trucks that might have been new thirty, forty, fifty years ago. It looked like the set of an old movie.

"Or maybe Small Compson," said Ronny, with a dark chuckle. "Oops, we missed it."

I think Abby and I both smiled at that. But Ronny was right, too. Even driving slowly, the village blurred past almost before it began. A handful of houses, a gas station, a grocery store, a diner, a stoplight. Then came half a mile of nothing before we saw a dirt area on the shoulder with a small store and an outdoor toilet off the back.

"Stop here," said Abby.

"Not yet," said Ronny. "We're almost —"

"Stop here!" Abby repeated.

Ronny slowed the car and pulled into the dirt lot. The rest stop had a run-down, sinister feel to it.

Like we didn't have enough of that already.

No sooner had Ronny turned off the engine than the little store's screen door filled with the shape of someone huge. I froze and listened closely, but I didn't hear any dead voices. At least not yet.

"I need a snack," Abby announced, hopping out of the car and heading for the store. "And a bathroom."

"You're not going in that store alone," I said.

"So come with."

I followed her across the lot. Abby was good-looking in a plain sort of way, and had the sort of sense of humor that Ronny was losing fast. I didn't mind going with her. But it was sweltering outside, and I was sweating like a hog. I hoped she wouldn't notice.

The big shape had disappeared by the time we reached the screen door. I pulled it open, it squealed, and we entered a tiny store stocked with dust and plenty of nothing else. Standing next to a warped linoleum counter was a large woman in a checkered dress, which hung all the way down to a pair of green rubber fishing boots on her feet. She gripped a sawed-off shotgun lightly, as if it were a toothpick.

"Uh . . . hi," I tried.

"Maybe," the woman said cautiously. "You city folk?"

I tried to grin. "We just came from Baton Rouge."

She hoisted the gun a little higher in her grip. "Pudge."

"Hey! That's not nice," said Abby. "Derek is getting thinner, actually —"

I turned to her. "I am?"

"*Name's* Pudge!" the woman interrupted. "Missy Pudge. People call me Missy."

"Oh," said Abby. Her cheeks flushed pink. Eager to change the subject, she nodded at an open display box on the counter. "Are these candy bars fresh?"

When Missy Pudge laughed, her face shook like pudding. "Would be, if this was 1977!"

Abby bought a peach.

"Wise choice," Missy said, still laughing and pocketing a quarter.

When Abby left to sample the outhouse, I was pretty sure I didn't want to stay in the store alone with the shotgun lady, so I headed outside, too. Ronny was still sitting in the car. I was going to wait with him when I caught sight of the long, dusty hood of a black car parked behind the store.

I stepped closer and saw that the big old car stretched almost the entire length of the store. It was built like a station wagon with a very long back compartment, but it wasn't really a car at all.

It was a hearse.

◄| FIVE |►

What Some Say

"Fifty-four Caddy," Missy said, coming up behind me and scratching a patch of gray whiskers on the tip of her chin. "Runs like a top. Hundred twenty miles an hour."

"Nice," I said, silently wondering why a hearse would need to go so fast.

Peering inside the back, I saw a high steel floor laid with runners and little wheels. I guessed that the wheels allowed coffins to slide in and out easily. Draped over the windows were faded velvet curtains tied with tasseled ropes of gold silk. Ornate lamps were mounted on each side, between the floor and ceiling.

"Are those lamps for the dead to read by?" I joked lamely.

"Ha!" Missy exploded with a cheek-wobbling laugh. "Now that's a funny picture! You know, this here limousine used to ferry the Longtempses from their house to the cemetery."

I shivered to hear a stranger mention my mother's family. Before I could say anything, words floated through my brain.

Ferry the dead, the many dead, the recent and the long dead.

"And what you're standing on," she went on, waving her shotgun across the air toward something other than trees and more trees, "this road, this rest stop, this whole land was once part of Amaranthia's Hundred. That's a hundred square miles stretching out from that big old house on both sides of the Red River. The town of Compson used to be on that property, too."

Was that why I had remembered the name?

"Big street in town is called Peace Road," she added, "on account of trying to heal after the riot."

"The riot?"

"Red Monday, 1921," she said. "In my daddy's daddy's day, that town was a hive of wicked folks. Guns, hijacking, killing, you name it. When agents finally came in to bust up the gang, some say they were even worse. Vengeful. Ruthless. Liquor stills exploded, fire swept the town. They call it Red Monday. In all, the riot killed close to two hundred folks, men, women, white, black, and all in between. The Longtempses helped rebuild Compson after. Since then, it's been called New Compson."

Death of two hundred people?

But by fire. Not by water. Maybe they were safe from the Legion.

Then Missy Pudge said, "All drowned."

My heart felt like it was going to fly out of my chest.

"But I thought —"

She laughed. "All comes down to the Red River, don't it? The inferno pushed the fighting all the way to the river. Some say you fight fire with water? Sometimes water don't want to help."

The idea trembled through me. I had to change the subject. "I'd like to see the big house," I said. "I like old houses."

"Ha! Some say the house lies eight, nine miles up the road on the far side of the river." She pointed a gnarled finger off among the oaks. "If you can find it, that is."

"Why wouldn't I be able to find it? It's a big house, isn't it?"

Missy rolled her lips in a strange way, as if she was hungry or surprised. "Folks around here sure don't go looking for it. If they do find it, it doesn't do them any good. Some say that house don't want finding!"

"But that's just some kind of legend, right?" I asked.

"Legend, nothing!" She spat on the ground next to my shoes, then scowled as if upset that she had missed. "I seen it firsthand! My daddy was a mason brought in to put new walks in the garden. From the moment he set foot there, he hated that house, and it hated him right back. Developers, contractors, workmen came and went. The lucky ones were run off by something or other. The unlucky ones just went insane."

Uh-huh. Right. So this was some scary backwoods movie filled with old hearses and nutty folks. Great. Just what I needed. And what was taking Abby so long? I wanted to get out of there.

"Is your father still around?" I asked, edging away slowly, toward Ronny and the car.

"Part of him," Missy said.

A shiver shot up my spine.

"His heart's still as strong as an ox. His mind's the thing that broke. Some say it's because of what he saw at that house one night. All I know is when you talk to him, he says just the one word."

I waited, but Missy Pudge just wiped her large cheeks with the back of her hand and turned away.

"What word?" I asked.

She swung back to face me. "Ghosts! That's the word. My daddy says nothing but 'ghosts' morning, noon, and night. One word is all."

I felt my knees quake.

"Derek —"

Ronny was scowling from the car window. "We have a lot to do." He started the engine. I nodded at Missy and climbed into the tiny car.

Abby finally joined us. "That restroom is no bigger than a coffin. I so want to take a shower."

"You can take five showers tomorrow," snapped Ronny, pulling away from the rest stop. "If we make it."

He slammed his foot on the gas and screeched out onto the road.

◄| SIX |►

The Riverbank

As Ronny raced up the road, his face set hard and eyes piercing the distance, pushing the little car to its limit, Abby leaned up and whispered in my ear.

"Cheery today, isn't he?"

I just nodded. I didn't feel so cheerful myself.

"Great," she muttered. "A couple of silent types." Abby tried to call her Grammy Nora, but reception was spotty. She settled back in her seat with a sigh.

There we were, alone in the middle of nowhere, in a stolen car, with dusk coming soon, looking for a haunted house.

Anyone want to switch places?

I didn't think so.

Over the next eight miles, I told Abby and Ronny about Red Monday and what Missy Pudge had said about the river and Amaranthia. Then Ronny slowed — to Abby's obvious relief — and we started looking for the red house. We couldn't see much. Both sides of the road were thick with oak trees.

"At least we got here before the Legion did," I said. "I usually hear them if they're nearby, but I don't hear anything. I guess we were faster —"

"You think we can win this thing?" Ronny snapped, cutting me off.

"What?"

His face was dark. "You think we can win this thing, don't you? You think the three of us clowns can win against the Legion. No one in the last hundred and fifty years has won against them. We're nothing. There's only one person who ever . . . who . . ." He drifted off.

I glanced at Abby, then back at him. "Ronny? There's only person who ever what?"

He hunched his shoulders, said nothing.

"Ronny?" I said. "Was there someone who fought the Legion and . . . won?"

Ronny glanced back at Abby in the rearview mirror. "What's he talking about?"

"Are you kidding?" she said. "Ronny, you started to tell us something. Did someone stop the Legion?"

"I don't know!" he burst out angrily, shaking his head over and over. "I don't know what you're talking about. Or what I'm talking about. I don't know what I was going to say. It's gone now. Stop asking —"

Before he could finish, I heard a shriek — or a hundred shrieks all at once — and a powerful wind blew out of the woods and sliced across the road. Ronny lost control of the wheel.

"Ronny!" Abby screamed.

The car shot into the ditch, then bounced back onto the road sideways. Ronny slammed on the brakes, which threw up a wall of dust around us.

"What was that —" I started to say.

Then an old green Jeep roared out of the dust, swerving to avoid us. Too late. Its bumper struck our left headlight hard. Glass splashed up into the dusty air. Both car and Jeep spun off into the ditch on the river side of the road.

Ronny twisted the wheel, stomping on the brake, but there was no stopping our car. It bounded down the embankment to the water before striking a tree. The front passenger door cracked open and I flew out, slamming against the ground. The weeds were thick where I fell, but my bad ear was crushed against a rock.

I howled.

Suddenly, almost in slow motion, the Jeep was bouncing down the bank toward me.

"Noooo —" I gasped.

I frantically tried to scramble out of the way, but the Jeep flipped over on its side. The driver screamed as it kept rolling toward me, its right tires spinning wildly.

A wagon's wheel spinning loose at twilight, round and round . . .

I tumbled down the bank to where a narrow stretch of river ran through the hollow at the bottom. Above, the Jeep's front tire caught on a stump, and it flipped now onto its roof, sliding at me backward. I jumped into the water and splashed across as fast as I could.

The Jeep hit the riverbank with a crash and stopped dead. The engine burst loudly.

"Ronny! Abby!" I yelled. No answer. They were far up the bank.

Smoke plumed from under the Jeep's hood. Ignoring it, I crawled to the cab. Inside, an older man with a grizzled face lay twisted across the wheel, his lips in the water, his arms tangled together as if pointing out the back window.

I knew there was nothing to do for him, but I couldn't let him stay like that.

I tried to pull him out, when something suddenly moved in the water outside the cab and splashed across the driver's face. A long, foul gasp blew out from his lips, his eyes bulged open, and his head jerked around.

I screamed.

He had been translated. And he had seen me.

My ear bleeding, I staggered away as quickly as I could. "Ronny! Abby!" I called again, hoping they weren't hurt, hoping they'd hear me. The dead soul groaned louder, angrier, thrashing inside the Jeep. I tried to climb up to the road, but a second storm of air rushed at my face, pushing me back into the water, sweeping me across it to the far side and up into the trees. I could barely see. I finally pushed my way through the thick wall of oaks on the embankment and out onto a vast field.

And there it was.

A giant hulk of a house, standing against the purple sky like a ghostly monument.

All the air in my lungs left at once.

Amaranthia.

◄ SEVEN ►

On the Fields of Defeat

Part of me knew I should turn away from the big red house, charge back through the trees across the water to Abby and Ronny, and tell them all about it.

But I didn't move.

Not in that direction, anyway.

I waded through the weeds toward the house, pulled, like I was in a movie and didn't have control over my character.

"This is not happening," I said to myself.

A step. Another step. Another.

I kept muttering. "That's a big old dark house, Derek. You shouldn't go there alone. Get a grip."

Step. Step. I realized I was soaking wet to my shoulders. I hadn't noticed before. The river must have been deeper than I'd thought.

I moved across the overgrown lawn, into the weaving threads of mist that rose from it. My ear bled, but the pain seemed dull somehow. Through it, I heard:

O scarlet walls, enwall from this nightmare war . . .

Yes! That was it! There was something comforting about the house. I was afraid of it, of course. A haunted house? An abandoned mansion? Anyone would be scared. But there was something hypnotic about the house, too. I wanted to be close to it.

I wanted to be inside it.

I found myself running across what must once have been the great lawn, toward the front steps, when a sound floated across the dusk into my bloody ear. I stopped to listen.

Was it music?

Or just the wind rustling the leaves?

There was no wind.

I heard strings being plucked. I heard bare feet walking on damp planks. I turned to my left and saw a row of cabins built of rough board that I hadn't noticed before. Each one had a peaked roof shingled in oak, and wood smoke rising from side chimneys. From my father's books I knew these were slave quarters, horrible things, but I remembered a story about them. Had Abby read it at the museum? No?

Then where had I heard it?

The story said that the slave houses at Amaranthia were not real slave quarters. The Longtempses used them to cover up what was really going on. At a glance, the family appeared no different from their slave-owning neighbors, but in fact it was smuggling blacks, hundreds of them, out of slavery to the far North of Ohio and Canada.

Had my mother told me this story?

I heard jangling strings and low crooning voices. I thought of Big Bob Lemon, and a lump thickened my throat. He was a huge man, indestructible — I had thought. There was something good and right about having Lemon on your side.

And yet, for all I knew, Bob had died two nights ago.

Another sound now, from my right, but this one clamored in my bad ear — the plinking of iron on iron. I recognized it as the battering of a hammer on an anvil.

Recognized it? When had I ever heard a blacksmith pounding an anvil? Never, that's when.

Still, my ear thudded with powerful hammer strokes, pounding out a slow, persistent rhythm. I saw the blacksmith's shop, a dark square of stone, its fireplace flickering orange. Beyond it were the long, low stables.

Out of the corner of my eye, I saw another light. Near the house.

Guttering like a failing candle-flame . . .

I swung around. There was no light. The red house was a dark shape. A dead thing.

My mind was playing tricks on me.

Then a movement in the garden. I saw a man.

Or was that a trick, too? Was it just the evening mist, twisting itself into shapes?

"Am I seriously seeing ghosts now?" I said, trying to laugh at myself. But would it have been so crazy?

I stepped closer.

The man had longish blond hair and wore a crisp gray uniform with a green sash at his waist that glinted in the moonlight. I watched him slide from a dark horse into the arms of a woman in white. Where had she come from? Her face was turned up to his, her long dress plumped out in front. Was she going to have a baby? The hydrangea bushes rustled, and the man turned.

Did I know him?

Was there a photo of him in the museum?

Among the bushes, five, six, or more uniformed riders took shape. Their faces were grim. They had to go.

Their horses' frightened eyes caught the yellow slanting moonlight. The man lowered his face to the woman's. Then, like some glitch in a movie, he was suddenly back on his horse again. He slid down like before, fell into her arms, pressed his face to hers, then was back on the horse.

This crazy, misty scene played over and over. It horrified me. But, beyond the fear, I couldn't help feeling very sad. What exactly was I watching? Was it a dream that wouldn't end? Ghosts caught in a treadmill of moments, unable to escape?

"Seeing ghosts now, Derek?" I said softly. "Just like old Missy Pudge's insane father? Is that what I am?"

No. No way.

I had to find Abby. Find Ronny.

Yet when I turned away from the garden, I found that I was only a few strides from the bottom of the main stairs.

I took in the house in an instant. It was like I had seen it every day of my life — the giant columns, the two galleries, one around the second floor and one around the top, just beneath the roofline.

The main gallery, a deck between the outer columns and the house, was ten feet deep, so the inside rooms wouldn't get direct sunlight. Columns extended from the floor up to the eaves on each side of the house. Two of the columns on a corner of the house had buckled, so the roof and the uppermost gallery sagged below the middle row of windows.

Why I went up the staircase, step by step to the top, I can't say. I don't even remember doing it. But somehow, I was there. The twin front doors, studded with big brass handles and decorated with amaranth carvings, stood right in front of me.

I knew I shouldn't. But I also knew that the old doors, heavy as iron, would swing open for me the instant I pushed. I just didn't know why. I took a deep breath, steadied my feet, and took hold of both handles.

A cry rang out across the lawn from the river.

"Derek! Derek!"

No, I thought. *Please go away.*

"Derek!"

Abby was hurrying toward the house, whipping her cane through the high weeds.

The spell broke like shattering glass. I couldn't hear the sounds from across the fields anymore. Only the dark souls' voices, their chorus of wails and groans, getting closer.

"The Legion —" I started.

"They're here!" Abby cried. "The Legion is attacking New Compson. They're burning it to the ground!"

Ronny wove across the open field in the beat-up car. The front end was bent back into itself, but it still ran. It spun out on the gravel in the garden where I saw no soldier or his wife.

Were they ever really there?

"Get in!" Ronny growled. "We have to help if we can."

Abby pulled me away from the house and pushed me into the back of the car. Ronny slammed his foot on the pedal. We tore across the field.

I looked back and saw that the blacksmith's shop was no more than a pile of stones, the slave houses toppled planks and weeds.

So.

Was it all just an illusion, after all?

Tires spitting up dust like a cyclone, we roared through the tall grass and into the trees.

◄ EIGHT ►

On Peace Road

Ronny angled the car between the hulking oak trees and onto a bridge he'd found buried among them.

Tangled trunks and branches crowded us on both sides, and I lost sight of Amaranthia. It felt as if part of me was still back on the steps of that red house. Would we be able to find the house again? Whatever my key opened was in that house. We had to find it. I had to go back.

But now, I could see a plume of black smoke rising up beyond the road and red flames licking the rooftops of burning houses. I heard the voices of the Legion screeching, moaning in my bad ear.

"There must be fifty of them by now," I said, trying to focus. "I hear them all. They've come for more victims. Missy Pudge said two hundred died on Red Monday, all drowned, escaping the fire."

"The duty of every soldier in the Legion is to grow the army," said Ronny, tearing into the rest stop again. "To do that, they have to supply bodies for the souls waiting to be translated. That's what they did in the bayou. That's what they're doing here." He opened the car door. "I saw some axes behind the rest stop."

Abby and I climbed out of the car and watched him go around the back of the store. He disappeared beyond the hearse, a black lump in the dwindling light.

"You know how to stop them?" I asked when he reappeared.

"I'm going to try," Ronny said, handing me an ax.

It was heavy in my hand, the head a big slab of sharpened steel. I remembered the blacksmith's shop at Amaranthia.

Ronny took an ax himself and held out a third one to Abby. She stepped back. "I have my cane," she said. "I'm not . . . not . . . using one of those things. I'm not a killer."

"They are," said Ronny, heading down the road without looking back, both axes over his shoulder. "All of them are killers. Maybe cutting them up will stop them." He paused. "Cutting . . . there's something I remember . . . something about the neck . . ."

"The *neck*?" Abby said, making a face.

Ronny jammed his eyes closed, then opened them. "There is a way to stop them. A horrible way. I'll remember it later. On foot from here. Be careful. Stay together. Let's go."

When we reached the village, it was a storm of chaos — worse than we'd imagined. New Compson was a grid of streets built around a central square and lined with a few stores, a diner, a gas station, a hotel. The dull shapes of the dead stormed here and there, heaving torches into houses and storefronts, driving the villagers out into the streets. People were screaming, running, staggering in the roaring white glow of the flames.

"Ronny, you know the Legion," said Abby, shielding her eyes from the heat. "How can we —"

"Try to stop any dead soldier you see!" Ronny cried, pointing at a group of five dead men in ragged shorts and T-shirts. I recognized them — tourists translated in Bayou Malpierre. "Hit them, cut them, trip them, slow them down. Do anything —"

A teenage boy ran over to us, carrying a gnarled stick. "Help us stop them!" he said. "I called the police!"

"They're coming from Bienville," shouted a uniformed man with wild hair, hurrying past with his pistol raised. "This is Red Monday all over again!"

As monstrous as the Legion soldiers looked — and you could tell which ones they were right away — they were methodical and calm. That was even more frightening.

"They have rifles in the hardware store!" a woman in a short dress called out. "We have to defend ourselves!" A moment later, a handful of men drove a car straight into the store, breaking the window.

The sound of shattering glass, the rush of water.

I shook my head. Not now.

Alarms sounded. The car reversed, and the crowd clambered over it to ransack the store for guns. I recognized Missy Pudge among them.

"The square!" a man shouted. "Get to the —" His voice was cut off. The heat fell over us like a wall. The sky was orange, white, black.

"Follow me," said Ronny, gripping an ax in each hand. "Don't split up." He turned to me. "I want to see you every minute." We hurried up Peace Road and into the square.

The hotel was on fire. Villagers massed at the Civil War monument on the green. They carried pitchforks, rakes, shotguns, chain saws, rifles. Ronny pushed his way into the center of the crowd.

"Look!" he said, trying to get everyone's attention. He jumped onto the hood of a car whose rear tires were burning. "The people attacking you are already dead. You can't kill them, you can only stop them from killing you! Don't go to the river! The dead come from the water. They want you there. They want you to drown —"

Two ambulances, a police car, and a fire engine screeched into the far side of the square. The dead swarmed them at once.

"He's one of them!" a voice yelled out, and someone threw something at Ronny, smacking his forehead. He slid to his knees on the car hood. Abby rushed to him.

"No!" I jumped up onto the car hood. "We're trying to —"

"Derek!" Abby cried, helping Ronny to his feet. "Tell them who you are!"

"What?" I didn't know what she meant. Then it hit me.

"I'm a Longtemps — Derek Longtemps Stone! That's my house over there. Amaranthia!"

Amid the inferno, the crowd hushed. In that hush, I heard the voice of Erskine Cane echoing in my bad ear. Three words.

He is here.

Cane meant me. I knew it.

The crowd stared at me, a hundred souls, black and white, men, women, and children. I had never been so frightened in my life.

"I —"

But I didn't get any further.

A pump at the gas station on the square exploded. I fell from the car. The crowd ran for cover.

The dead — fifty or more — charged after us, howling. Their voices crashed into my ear.

"This way," said Ronny.

The three of us scrambled behind the diner, which had escaped the fire so far. Old tires, the crumpled fender of a truck, and three cracked radiators were strewn on the ground. Overturned garbage. Rats.

I dropped to my knees, exhausted. Cane's steely voice stung my bad ear again. *Take them from their houses. He is here.* Then the sound of engines, low and rough, as trucks were driven straight into houses — glass exploded, wood snapped, the roaring engines popped from the heat.

And voices, screaming: "To the river! Save yourselves from the fire! To the river!"

"No, no," said Ronny, over and over and over.

The sound of shattering glass, the rush of water.

We raced out from behind the diner again, desperate to help, and it all stopped.

People ran, houses burned, Ronny and Abby yelled, but for me it stopped when I saw them.

Erskine Cane. Twitchy. Waldo Fouks.

I stood amid the chaos of Peace Road, and I couldn't move. Cane had just spoken, but Twitchy went running off with a torch as if he didn't hear. All at once, Cane spun forward and wrapped his massive arms around Twitchy's head. Cane twisted his arms swiftly. I gagged as Twitchy squirmed and uttered a long groan. I saw something come rushing out of the back of his head like a patch of dark air. There was a shriek, then Twitchy went still. The big soldier opened his hands, and the body fell, dark and unmoving, to the middle of the road.

Waldo's blind eyes squinted skyward. He was shaking. "You cut him. . . ."

And now I'd seen how the animated dead die. Ronny was right. It was horrible.

"The First has called me," said Cane. "I rule here."

Whatever jumble of ideas, questions, and nightmares I'd had about the Legion was clarified in that instant, when I saw Cane and Waldo on the street.

Maybe there was the First, but right now the dead had only one leader.

Ruthless, stark, deadly, Cane towered over the blind boy and spoke. "The First has commanded. Grow the Legion, stop the young captain. I hear the enemies. They are close. Three of them. The boy has the key."

The young captain?

He turned to a handful of dead men, some of whom were Waldo's smugglers. One by one, they nodded.

"Take the humans to the river," Cane said to Waldo.

"Use the trucks. I will burn the red house. The First has commanded it."

Cane spoke in a slow monotone, as if each word was carefully thought out.

I was frozen where I stood. No one saw me.

I watched Cane stomp away, knowing I'd just seen the brutal leadership of the Legion.

I hadn't seen the First, but Cane blindly obeyed him, and that frightened me more than anything else I'd seen so far.

And *three* enemies? He was talking about us. Ronny, sure. He was translated. And I already knew if my bad ear allowed me to hear the dead, somehow the dead could hear me. But Abby? How could he hear Abby? Or was it someone else? Who was the third?

"Ronny!" I whispered over my shoulder. "Abby!"

No answer.

Waldo shrieked orders to a handful of the dead, fear dripping from his blind eyes. The Legion soldiers dragged victims into the trucks. They were headed for the river where — I knew — the untranslated dead, the killers and hijackers, had been waiting since Red Monday. To return.

I staggered away, found Ronny and Abby in the empty streets.

"He knows we're here," I told them. "We need to get to the house. Cane's going to burn it. I have to find what the key opens now!"

Ronny growled.

"Derek's right," Abby said softly. "We need to go to Amaranthia."

"Then there's nothing more for us here," Ronny said finally.

We looked only long enough to see the dead moving toward the river, their faces blackened, their clothes smoking, their eyes focused on some horrible future.

The soldiers were doing their duty. The Legion was growing. How many would there be by nightfall? A hundred? Two hundred?

More?

◄| NINE |►

To the Red House

We tore up the road toward Amaranthia, the car rattling like it might fall to pieces at any minute. Ronny didn't seem to care if he made it worse by driving like a crazy person, until two tires blew. The car finally died for good in a roadside ditch.

"Oh, man, oh, man, oh, man," Abby said under her breath.

Ronny climbed out and kicked the flat tires. "We'll have to hoof it from here."

"Take the hearse," I said, pointing back toward the rest stop. "It's our only chance to get there before the Legion."

Ronny looked back. "Fine. Hurry."

We hustled along the road, hearing the wail of sirens racing up from the south.

When we reached the rest stop, I searched the store and found Missy Pudge's keys below the register. I was a regular car thief now. Fantastic. Ronny had taught me well.

We wrenched open the hearse doors. They squealed like the voices of the dead. Appropriate. We climbed in, and Ronny started the engine. It rumbled to life. He jerked the stick into reverse, and we pulled onto the road with a shriek of rubber.

We raced up the road in silence, passing the junked car, then passing the green Jeep in the embankment. I sensed it was empty. The dead driver had freed himself.

We drove along the bank for a while, then veered narrowly between two trees and over the bridge Ronny had found before.

I felt dizzy and drained as we rolled over the old stones toward the house.

Stone road, cold road, road to time long past . . .

I hated the words in my head. "Faster," I said. "Missy said this car can could do a hundred twenty miles an hour."

"Not through the woods it can't," Ronny said. Less than a minute later, he jerked the hearse to a stop in the weeds, a hundred feet from the red house.

"Inside, before they get here," he instructed.

"Flashlights?" Abby asked. "It'll be dark in there."

Ronny shrugged. "Try the glove box."

She banged the glove compartment open with the heel of her hand. "Two," she said. "In case they need to bury someone at night, I guess. Only one of them works."

"Bring it," said Ronny. "There are probably candles inside, if the rats haven't eaten the wax. We need to find what that key opens, then scram. Cane and the others will be here soon. I want to be long gone when they show up."

My head was a fog. When the two of them climbed out of the hearse, I sat staring at the red house like a kid at his first drive-in movie. I couldn't move.

"Get out," said Ronny sharply.

Of course. I knew I had to.

But I also knew that the moment I set foot inside Amaranthia, I would be lost to it. I would be in that trance again. Seeing things. Hearing voices. I was scared to death. Of the house. Of Cane. Of everything. Why couldn't I move?

O scarlet walls, enwall from this nightmare war . . .

"Get out," Ronny repeated. "The Legion will be here so fast, your head will spin."

"Okay," I said. I thought of Twitchy's head. I still couldn't move.

"Or just stay there and give me the key —"

"Back off, soldier," said Abby, flashing Ronny a look. She reached into the car and pulled my arm gently. "Derek, we don't have time for this. Come on."

Drawing a long breath, I slid off the seat, moved toward the stairs and those giant front doors. The hammering of horseshoes, the strumming of guitars, the warbling voices across the fields — they were nothing now. Darkness and silence. Scattered stones, loose bricks, weeds. The soldier and his young wife were only mist in the moonlight.

Ronny was pacing the high grass like a madman. He finally clamped his hand on my arm and pulled both Abby and me onto the stairs. We all went up together.

At the top they stepped aside, and for the second time I took the door handles in my shaking fingers.

But this time I turned them and pushed. The doors swung in, and the house gasped out a stale breath of welcome.

◄ TEN ►

Dead Air

The air, thick and heavy, was worse than no air at all. My throat stung. I barely breathed.

I don't know why, but I had an overwhelming urge to shut the doors and seal us off from the outside world. No sooner had we stepped through them than I took hold of the inside knobs and pushed the doors closed.

"Okay, this isn't going to turn into some creepy teen movie, is it?" Abby said, flicking on her flashlight.

"No." I paused. "It's been a creepy teen movie for a month already."

She narrowed her eyes at me, then shone her light into the dark house.

The first thing we saw was a staircase, sweeping up from the entryway in a wide curve. The walls on either side were hung with faded portraits. Confederate soldiers. Young women. Old women with faces dry as paper, dressed in black. They were widows, I knew. I had seen them in my father's Civil War books, dressed in what were called "widows' weeds" — black dresses, black bonnets, white lace at the neck and wrists. Had all their husbands died in the war?

"Look for something small," said Abby, bringing me crashing back to reality.

"It's not going to be easy," Ronny said darkly. "The rooms are mostly empty. Looted by squatters, probably."

"A chest. A box. A drawer," she went on. "Maybe even a wall panel. This house is probably full of secret passages. Look for anything with a lock on it."

"We should split up," said Ronny. "This house has thirty rooms, at least. Besides, the voices are getting closer. I hear Waldo's crazy shrieking. They'll be here soon."

Ronny could hear the voices of the Legion. In some part of my head, I could hear them, too, just as I had since the train accident. But there were other sounds now. Other voices. And not just those crazy lines of poetry that kept popping in for a visit. Voices I hadn't heard before. Old voices, chanting from the darkness.

You . . . see . . . you . . . see . . .

I looked at Ronny and Abby to check if they heard them, too. They didn't react. Great. Like Waldo Fouks said, I'm special.

I shook my head to clear the voices, but they only got sharper, more insistent.

You . . . see . . . !

See what? Maybe my hurt ear was playing more tricks on me. Why not? Load it on. Make me crazier than I already am.

Plink . . . plink . . .

Through a cracked door to the right, I saw the shambles of what I somehow knew was the everyday parlor. The wreck of an ancient upright piano leaned against the wall. Its keys sounded randomly, as if fingered by ghostly hands. The sound made me shiver.

Plink . . . plink . . .

Then I spotted a large gray mouse, hobbling on three legs back and forth across the keys.

"What? No ghost?" Abby said shakily, trying to be funny.

No one laughed.

I thought of the soldier and his bride in the garden. Were they really ghosts? Had I really seen them at all?

"Yuck," Abby went on, filling the silence. "This place makes me want to shower for a week. Here's a candle. You take it." Using matches on the table next to it, she lit it. I took the candlestick.

"Get moving, you two," Ronny snarled. "I'm going upstairs. Whoever finds something, yell. And Derek, have the key ready. Don't lose it in the dark, all right?"

"He won't lose it," Abby scoffed. Then she turned to me and whispered, "Do not lose that key!"

We split up at the bottom of the big staircase. Abby headed left, Ronny went up the steps, and I walked straight ahead, underneath the curving stairs.

I had no idea what I would find that way, but going under the stairs seemed right somehow. I took a step, another, under the stairs and around a corner into the north wing of the house. The whole way, the air was like wool, suffocating and heavy.

Then the scratching started.

It came from behind the wall to my right, and it sounded like fingernails scraping on wood. I jerked away, cringing, and the scratching was behind me. Then it was beneath the floor at my feet, as if something were looking up through the boards.

The voices were back. Whispers, hissings, all in my bad ear.

You . . . see . . . you . . . see . . .

"I don't see! Get away from me!" I must have hit my ear harder than I thought in the car crash.

I hurried back — I thought — to where Abby was. The darkness and shadows confused me, and I didn't find her. But the scratches found me, scuttling behind the old wood like an army of rats. My skin crawled. Was someone there? Was the house alive?

I found a small room, a little office no bigger than a pantry. It smelled like oil and dead flowers. A broken chair and a small table draped with a rug sat under a window.

I checked the table for drawers. It had none, but a pair of eyes flashed out from under the draped rug. I'm not proud of it, but I think I screamed. A shape the size of a cat skittered out from beneath the table.

A raccoon.

Surprised by me, too, the raccoon jumped back under the table. I kicked the table legs, expecting the creature to run past me to the hallway. But it didn't. There was only a muffled scuffling in the wall behind the table as the animal hurried away.

I pulled the table away from the wall, its legs shrieking against the floorboards. The raccoon was nowhere in sight. In the candlelight, I saw that the wall panel behind the table was hinged. The raccoon had disappeared behind it.

I pried it open.

A passage ran the length of the house behind the wall. I held up the candle and saw struts, planks, studs, and bricks disappearing into the distance. An occasional round piece of glass, like the bottom of a flat bottle, was set in the walls, and clouded moonlight fell into the length of the passage.

I knew it was a bad idea, but I couldn't stop myself. I stumbled forward on boards at first, then stone, as the passage dipped below the level of the first floor of the house. Sour air wafted up from somewhere below.

Glass shattered on the floor above me. "Derek?" It was Abby, muffled and far away.

"Abby?" I said. She couldn't have heard, I was so quiet. Like in the bayou, I couldn't raise my voice.

I was quiet, but the passage was breathing with voices.

Forward!

Come!

Go!

One rumbly old voice reminded me of Bob Lemon's. *Never, no, never . . .*

Then several women's voices rose over the others, chanting those words again. *You . . . see . . . you . . . see . . .* It was a chorus, moving in and out like waves at the shore. Other voices broke through, all of them burbling in the darkness.

Who are you, boy?

Don't steal our silver, please, it's all we have —

We have waited so long, so very long . . .

And again: *Who are you, boy?*

"Enough!" I cried, pushing past them. By the time I reached the end of the passage, I was a good two feet lower than where I started. I froze. In my candle's glow I could see a set of stairs leading down into darkness.

Then I saw a hand. A hand? No. There was nothing there. I was imagining it. I leaned onto the top step, steadied myself on the banister.

I felt something brush the hair on the back of my hand.

"No. No way," I whispered. Closing my eyes, I imagined another hand placing itself lightly upon the banister. It was a woman's, old, shriveled, white, a fringe of lace at the wrist. A widow's hand. It slid down the banister slowly.

"This is crazy!" I said aloud, opening my eyes and seeing nothing. But it was happening. I knew it. I was being sucked into this weird old house, hearing things, seeing things. Impossible things. Ghosts.

Two old shapes formed, three, four, their shrunken white faces marked with the black smudge of death, their cheeks carved with silver tears.

The Widows' Pledge! said one. Then a second voice

joined in, then all of them, a chorus of old voices. *The Widows' Pledge!*

I knew they weren't really there, but in my mind they were all around me. We descended the stairs together, a parade of widows and me. They were chanting, over and over.

You . . . see . . . you . . . see . . .

"No, I still don't see," I whispered. My throat felt like sandpaper.

Step by step by step, I went down the stairs, until my foot struck the floor with a thud. Moonlight, silver and pale, fell on a network of arches and columns surrounding a big white stone house.

So that was it.

I had found the crypt.

◁| ELEVEN |▷

What the Key Opens

I was in the basement of the house. The floor was laid with brick, but it was uneven, as if the bricks were set directly on the ground. Big wooden beams supported the floor above.

Moonlight filtered down from small barred windows high in the walls, and I saw tattered cobwebs hanging over the white stone tomb.

It was a crypt, like the others I'd seen in recent days — in St. Louis Cemetery in New Orleans, in the ancient boneyard in Bayou Malpierre. It smelled like water and death and age.

. . . that bitter perfume of death.

Good thing I hadn't eaten all day.

Somewhere in the dark — or in my mind — I heard the widows murmur again.

"Quiet, already," I said, but I'd said it so softly I wondered if I'd actually said it aloud.

I gripped the candlestick. I wanted to feel it pinch

the softness of my fingers and wake me from this gauzy dream.

"I'm Derek Stone!" I insisted to myself. "I hate this stuff. Up is up! Down is down! I don't believe in ghosts."

But nothing changed.

The widows murmured on. *You . . . see . . .*

The tomb walls were carved with the same flower design I'd seen on everything else in the house. Amaranths. Only here, black mold had crawled inch-thick over the stone, pitting the alabaster.

Fixed on the crypt door was a small gilt oval frame and, inside it, an old photograph of a young man, a soldier.

With light locks dangling to his shoulders, a thin mustache, and a beard on his chin, he looked solemnly at the camera. On his shoulders were epaulets and tassels.

It was the same soldier I had seen in the garden. But how did I know what he looked like before even seeing the photograph? And who was he, anyway?

The widows hushed their mumbling for a second, then started again.

In the photo the young man was stern-faced. But for some reason, I imagined him smiling, moving, alive, and — oddly — I imagined his hair parted on the other side.

"Whatever," I said to the dark. I really was losing it.

The stone door of the crypt had a handle mottled with green rust. I turned it, pulled it toward me. The big white door slid open easily.

Not a good sign.

The widows' murmuring grew louder.

Inside the tomb, on a high stone pedestal, lay a black oak coffin. Its lid was just above eye level.

Holding my shrinking candle high, I made myself enter the crypt. Starting on the right, I walked completely around the dusty coffin until my legs refused to move anymore. From there, I could see a brass plate with the same amaranth design as the key in my pocket. The plate had a slot in it, a lock, set into the coffin just under the edge of the lid.

I breathed out.

So this was it. The coffin of some hundred-and-fifty-year-old dead guy I didn't even know?

"But the key might not work," I said aloud, trying to make sense of it all. "It might not even work on this lock."

Only I couldn't stop my fingers from running over

the delicate scrollwork surrounding the lock. I knew I had to try it.

While the widows murmured on — *You*... *see*... — I pulled the old key from my pocket and slowly slid it into the lock.

It went in all the way to the handle.

My chest froze, my stomach throbbed.

Somewhere, in the corner of my mind, I heard footsteps tramping across the floor over my head. *Thump. Thump.* I thought of Abby. Was she searching for me — or running for her life? Never mind. I had to do this. I couldn't leave yet.

Resting the candlestick on the coffin lid, I gripped the key firmly and turned.

The lock clicked.

◄ TWELVE ►

The Red Stain

I stood motionless by the coffin for a long time. The only sound I heard was the echo of that *click*.

Placing the candlestick on the corner of the pedestal, I took the lid of the casket in both hands and lifted as far as I could until, with a muffled squeak, it stayed open. The air inside was stale, old, dry. I tried not to breathe it in.

Shreds of satin lining hung like silver moss from the inside of the lid. At first, nothing was visible over the top. My heart skipped. Was the coffin empty? Maybe the key meant nothing at all.

But I had to look inside.

Standing on my toes, I peered over the edge of the casket, and my stomach flipped. Inside was a uniform of rags. A fleshless skull was tipped back on the sunken remains of a sickly brown pillow. Crumbled vertebrae snaked into the woolen collar of a military jacket. My throat thickened. It was disgusting. But I couldn't take my eyes away. Was this all that remained of the bright young man in the photograph? The gallant soldier in the garden?

"Who are you?" I said softly.

The widows' voices paused again, but only for an instant.

The bones of his fingers were folded over his sunken chest in the same way as knights I'd seen in cathedral crypts. But clutched between them was something wrapped in a faded green cloth. I knew it was the sash — emerald green silk trimmed with a half-disintegrated shred of gold tassel — of a Civil War cavalry officer. I'd seen photos of those sashes in my dad's old books, and the soldier had worn it in the garden.

The sash was folded tightly around something the size of a small, flat box. I couldn't tell you why, but my fingers itched to hold the thing, whatever it was. And, weirdly, I felt as if the chanting widow ladies echoing in my crazy, jumbled head expected me to take it.

Had they led me down here for just that reason?

So now I was doing what ghosts wanted me to? Yeah, I was far gone, all right.

I gently slid the object out from under the fleshless fingers. I pressed it against my own chest and stepped away from the coffin, lowered the lid, locked it, pocketed the key. Taking my candle, I walked backward out of the crypt, feeling like the thing I had found, whatever it was, was what I'd been searching for my whole life.

Standing in a pale blade of moonlight, I carefully unwrapped the sash. Inside was a leather pouch — scratched, worn, and as brittle as old wood. A flap over the top was snapped in place. When I unwound its narrow leather straps, I recognized the pouch as a Civil War cartridge box.

The letters CSA were stamped into the flap.

"Confederate States of America," I said to myself.

So what was inside? Old rifle shells? Pistol bullets? Ammunition to use against the Legion?

No.

I snapped open the cartridge box carefully. Inside was a small, leather-bound book with an amaranth design pressed into the leather. I lifted the cover of the book. Snaked across the first page, from bottom left to top right, was a dark stain tinged with red. Dried blood.

Written in a dense black scrawl across the page, I read:

The Ghost Road
A Poem of the Long War
by
Capt. Ulysses Perceval Longtemps

Captain? Erskine Cane had said he was searching for the young captain.

I didn't breathe, I couldn't, as I ran my fingers across the inked words.

Ulysses Perceval Longtemps . . .

The name shivered through me. He was a relative, okay, but had I ever heard the name before? As far as I could remember, I hadn't. But in my mind, the name sounded like the shattering of glass and the long drawn notes of a violin.

"Ulysses Perceval Longtemps . . ." I said aloud, barely a whisper.

All at once I sensed the widows emerging from the shadows, floating closer to me. Then again, in that room of death, the quivering moonlight made it seem like everything was moving. They murmured their words over and over, and I finally understood. They weren't saying *you . . . see . . . you . . . see . . .* at all. They were saying *Ulysses.*

But why? My throat went dry.

I turned the page over to the beginning of the long poem, and read its first words:

Within your crimson walls, I was an angel child . . .

Blood drained from my head. I wobbled.

I knew those words! I'd heard them over and over in my mind since the train wreck. Seeing them here in my hands, I felt like I was being pulled overboard. And I remembered the next lines as I read them:

From room to room I floated in your wingless window light,

And yet gray Evil, like a wolf, from shadows sprang . . .

I snapped the book closed.

"No!" I shouted to the darkness. "I can't know these stupid words —"

There was a scuffling sound on the dusty floor above. The voices vanished like fog in a wind. My candle blew out, and the pale moonlight clouded over outside, plunging the crypt black.

"Derek?" came a whisper.

I jumped. Was this voice real? Or ghostly, like the others?

"Derek?"

It came from the top of the wooden stairs. "Derek, are you down there in the dark?"

"Abby?" I said softly, still dazed.

"Derek!" she cried, sounding relieved. "Is Ronny with you?"

"Ronny?" It took me a moment. "No. He's not —"

"Then get up here fast," she said. "He's gone. I think the Legion is already in the house, and they've got him —"

"They've got . . ." I said, unbelieving. Footsteps thudded on the floorboards. Ronny's bloodcurdling scream cut through the dead air of the room.

"Ronny!" I shouted.

I swallowed a thousand questions, stuffed the book and sash into the cartridge box, slung it over my shoulder, and hurried up the stairs to Abby. The spell of the crypt was shattered.

"I'm coming!"

⊲ THIRTEEN ⊳

On the Gallery

Crashing, yelling, feet pounding through the passage. Abby grabbed my arm and wouldn't let go, pulling me up the stone steps after her.

"You found something?" she said breathlessly, eyeing the pouch slung over my shoulder.

"A book," I said, already winded. You'd think I would have gotten better at this whole running-from-the-dead thing by now.

"What book?"

"How did you find me?" I asked, pushing off the question. "How —"

"I . . ." she started. "I don't know. I just knew you were down there. This house. My mother."

"Your mother?" I said, still struggling to keep up. The girl with the cane was faster than me.

"There's some connection between us. Don't ask me how, but for some reason, I usually know where you are. This is so completely not the way my life is supposed to go —"

She glanced back at me. "What's the book?"

I didn't know how to explain it, the words in my head, the words in the book.

"Derek, hello? You still in there?"

I shook my head. "Later. Later!"

We rushed out of the passage, through the little study, and out under the stairs. Abby stifled a scream.

A man whose clothes hung in charred tatters stood in the main hall. A New Compson townsman — translated. His head swiveled toward us, toward me, toward the pouch. A grin. Black teeth.

"Found!" he cried.

Pushing Abby ahead of me up the stairs, I stumbled and fell back into the guy. The smell from his open mouth was nauseating. I kicked wildly, catching him in the shoulder, and Abby swung her cane at his head. He fell back, eyes bulging in anger.

"This way!" Abby called, yanking me up the stairs with her.

Ronny's cries were moving quickly, somewhere far above us. We rushed up another flight of stairs to the top floor.

"Ronny!" We threw ourselves at the nearest door. It popped open in time for us to see a troop of dead men drag Ronny through a window onto the balcony outside. Waldo was barking orders at them.

"Get out there!" I yelled, lunging for the window.

"No! No," said Abby. "This way!" She pulled me back to the hallway.

"What — Abby —"

"This way!" she insisted. "Cut them off."

I followed her down the hallway. She pushed through door after door until we reached the side of the house. The gallery outside was empty.

"He's not here," I said.

Her face was odd, twisted. "This is where we should . . . let's get outside —"

"How do you —"

"She's here. My mother. With Ronny. I know it." Abby tried the windows. They were hopelessly stuck. I cast around and saw a poker in the fireplace. With both hands, I swung it hard at the nearest window, then ran it around the edges to break whatever wooden slats and glass remained.

We scrambled through the window onto the gallery outside. It squealed with our weight, sagging between us and the corner.

"This won't hold us," I said. "It's going to break —"

But there he was.

Ronny was held up limply by a handful of Legion soldiers, Waldo at their head. My brother's face was a mask of terror, his legs twisted under him. His eyes fell on the cartridge box, and he knew. "Derek, don't say anything! Nothing! Get that out of here!"

"I knew you would find it," Waldo squeaked. How did he know? His blank eyes searched my face. "You really are a special Longtemps, aren't you? Now give it to me, or we cut the boy from his soul."

Cut. I could tell by Ronny's face that he must have remembered what it meant to be cut.

"We're not leaving you, Ronny," I said, still holding the poker. "And you're not getting this, Waldo."

Waldo's blind eyes drilled into mine. Behind him were some of the dead villagers from New Compson. Their faces were wet, gray, smoking. I knew they had drowned at the river.

Waldo nodded his little head, and a Legion soldier knocked Ronny in the chest. My brother fell limp to the gallery floor.

"You —" I stepped forward, Abby next to me. The planks under our feet cracked loudly.

"Give us what you found," Waldo commanded. I felt for the cartridge box hanging at my waist.

What you found? So he didn't know what it was?

"No," I said as calmly as I could. I took Abby by the arm. A dark shape moved behind Waldo. I smelled decay and knew who it was.

Erskine Cane's wife.

In the body of Abby's mother.

Even before she got a clear view of her mother, Abby began wobbling. "Oh, no . . ."

"I'm sorry. I should have told you," I whispered.

"Cut the boy," Waldo ordered.

"No!" I said. My heart turned to ice as Abby's mother slid out from behind Waldo. She was worse than before. Her legs were no larger or stronger than planks of old wood beneath her ragged dress. Her arms were rods of white bone, her face draped with flesh the color of dirty milk.

But she hoisted Ronny's limp body in one powerful arm. Her gray hands clamped his head. Ready to twist? To cut him?

"No!" I burst out. "Here it is, take it —"

I moved to throw the book to Waldo, but Abby's mother pushed forward, screeching in my ears like a teapot ready to explode. "First! Find the — First! One day only — one day!"

Abby gasped. "She's talking to *you*, Derek."

All at once, with inhuman strength, her mother hurled Ronny across the sagging gallery at us. Waldo wailed and lunged at the woman with his creepy little hands, like he was going to cut her himself. She wriggled free and threw herself onto the lowest part of the gallery, splintering the planks between us. It started to rip away from the house.

Without thinking, I smashed the window next to me with the poker. Not knowing where I got the strength, I pushed Ronny through to the room inside.

"Abby, get back!" I shouted as the boards cracked beneath our feet.

"Mom!" Abby cried, reaching out for her mother. Their hands touched. The wood splintered. The railing snapped.

"Get in here!" I screamed. I threw one arm tightly around Abby's waist and pushed her through the window, falling in after her.

Waldo and the others skittered back to the corner as the gallery plummeted away from the house, taking Abby's mother to the ground with it.

Abby was screaming and trembling like a leaf on the floor of the room. All at once, she jumped to the window. We saw her mother's motionless shape on the ground. Her face gray with horror, Abby cried out over and over, "Mom! Mommy!"

Then her mother moved. She twisted on the ground like a wounded animal, then jerked awkwardly to her feet, and, with a single look back at Abby, stomped away toward the woods. She picked up speed, finally running away from the house until she was gone.

"She's —" Abby started, then broke down in tears.

"Come on," I managed to say, pulling her toward the door and dragging Ronny to his feet. "We have to go."

◄ FOURTEEN ►

Wings of a Carved Angel

Coming to and spotting the cartridge box slung over my shoulder, Ronny was suddenly as alert as a soldier in battle.

"Downstairs!" he barked. "We have what we need. Let's go!"

We barreled after him. Abby was still sobbing, but she kept up as best she could. "She escaped. She's out there. Derek, my mother's out there!"

"I know," I said.

I didn't know where her mother would go or what she would do, only that she had saved Ronny.

And the book.

Ronny led us down to the second-floor landing. We'd planned to get all the way out of the house, but we pulled up short.

Erskine Cane stormed out from a side hall with the gray-haired man, the one-armed conductor, and a dozen others, blocking our way. He held an unlit torch. On him, a torch was more terrifying than a cannon.

"I want the book!" he demanded, stomping toward us like a machine.

He knows it's a book, I thought. *What else does he know?*

Ronny grabbed the poker that I'd been too distracted to put down, and threw it at Cane's head — not doing any damage, just distracting him.

"Run!" Ronny said, reaching for Abby's hand. "The back hall!"

He and Abby took off with me close behind. I followed the sound of their footsteps in the dark, stumbled, the dead stomping after me. Soon I heard only my own footsteps. I slowed.

"Ronny? Abby?" I whispered.

No answer.

What part of the house was I in now?

I tried to breathe slowly, clutched for the cartridge box. Still there. But Ronny and Abby were nowhere. Or maybe I was nowhere.

A draft of cool air brushed my cheek, and I turned to face it.

This way . . .

Them again. The voices. I didn't want to listen, but the hallway behind me suddenly thudded with footsteps, so I slipped into a tall room. It was empty except for a cast-iron staircase, narrow, with a busted railing only halfway up. It led to a ceiling a good twenty feet high.

I pushed the door closed behind me. The stomping feet of the dead passed. Why hadn't they heard me?

You are both with us . . .

Both?

The staircase creaked, quivered in the still air. Was I supposed to go up the stairs?

Beyond the top step, I saw a door. Was someone behind it?

Come . . . come . . . you . . . see . . .

Was it his room?

Was it Ulysses Longtemps's room?

I set my foot on the first iron step. The whole staircase swayed under my weight. It was like stepping onto a boat. It made me dizzy, but I climbed up the spiral stairs, round and round, higher and higher. The closer I got to the top, the more clearly I saw that the stairs had broken away from the landing. Every step I took pulled them farther from the wall.

When I reached the top, I hoisted myself off the uppermost step and onto the small landing.

I pushed the door. It opened onto a small, windowed room at the very top of the roof, like the *faux chambre* in my old house in New Orleans. The house that Erskine Cane burned down. It seemed like so long ago since I had been there, even though it had only been a few days.

Was this my life now? Running? Hiding? Would it ever stop moving long enough for me to understand it?

Red damask curtains, looking as heavy as iron sheets, draped the walls between the windows. Almost every window was broken, letting in the gauzy yellow moonlight and hot night air.

On either side of an empty mantelpiece was a place for an ornament. On the right one stood a carved angel, painted gold. I knew that angel. The left space was empty.

So.

The golden angel where the key had been hidden had come from this room. The angel on top of my house in New Orleans had once been here. But why? I dug in my pocket for the key, clutched it tight.

I could never have been in this little room before. Of course not. But I knew it was Ulysses Perceval Longtemps's room. Without thinking, I bent down to a panel on the left of the door. My fingers found a small gash that I knew had been made when Ulysses was sixteen and practicing saber. He had cut his arm that day.

I suddenly wanted to get out of there. This was all too much. I wanted my mind back.

Hushhhhh.

The flowery scent of magnolia wafted through the room. It brought me back to the museum. I'd smelled it there, and long before that, too.

In my mind, I saw the narrow streets of the City of the Dead, St. Louis Cemetery in New Orleans, ten years earlier. The ghost scent of magnolia had floated there, too. I remembered my little hand held firm in another's warm grip.

The floorboards creaked, and the fragrance fell over me. Had it drifted into the room through the windows?

No. It wasn't from outside.

A whisper of movement, the sound of fabric drawn aside, and I wasn't alone.

◀ FIFTEEN ▶

Just Like Old Times

A shape moved from shadow to shadow, and soon a face framed by long black hair formed in the moonlight.

The scent of magnolia bloomed in the small room.

"Who are you?" I asked.

No answer. But I knew.

The shape took a step, cutting into the pale light.

My throat tightened. "Who —"

"Derek, honey . . ."

I froze inside. Said nothing.

"Derek, honey, it's me."

I said nothing. Nothing. And then . . .

"Mom?"

"I'm here, honey."

It all came out in a rush of words. "Mom? Mom! What are you doing here? I haven't seen you for ten years. And . . . your perfume! I smelled it at the museum this morning, before the explosion. It was you. You were there! But you're supposed to be in France. Dad said you were in France —"

"Derek, your father —"

"And before that," I interrupted. "I smelled it in the cemetery when I was young. I remember."

"Derek, your father . . ." she repeated softly, then stopped.

"Dad? What about Dad?" My father's face swam in my mind. I imagined his damaged hand, his deep, tired eyes. I didn't know how he had survived the train wreck — I didn't know if he really had. And here was my mother, after ten years, talking about him. "What about Dad?"

"Don't . . ."

She stopped again.

"Don't what? Mom. Tell me."

"Don't trust him, Derek. He was at the war memorial. He's been following you. I —"

"Following me?" I practically screamed, shaking all over. "What are you talking about? Are you serious? Don't trust *him*? I don't trust you!" I heard yelling from the floors below, echoing footsteps. "You left me, Mom. You ran away. I was only four. Don't trust *him*? You can't be serious —"

"Deadly serious, Derek. I had to keep him away from you. The explosion —"

"That was you?" I said. "But how?"

"I had to keep him away from you, Derek. And I've come here to tell you why."

"This is crazy," I spat. My hands grabbed at the air in front of me, as if trying to shake something loose. Then I felt the key, cutting into my palm.

"This old key," I said slowly. "You hid it in the angel on the roof in New Orleans, didn't you? You put it there."

"The key was hidden in that angel long ago, Derek, by someone other than me." Her eyes glanced at the empty spot next to the mantel. "I had it put on the roof when your father decided to turn the *faux chambre* into his room. It would be safe up there until it was needed."

She spoke as if we had talked every morning and night for the last ten years. I hadn't laid eyes on her that whole time, hadn't heard her voice on the telephone, hadn't seen so much as a photograph of her.

"Needed? What for? To find this book?"

She put her hands out, palms up. "This is where he was laid out, you know. His things were right here, where we're standing."

My mind was a storm of questions.

"Ulysses loved it up here," she went on before I could get anything out. "The Finial, he called it. 'I'm going up to the Finial now,' he'd say. 'I'll be in the Finial until dinnertime.' He was like that."

I was shaking all over. "You talk like you knew him."

Her black hair stirred in some movement of air I didn't feel. "Ulysses Perceval Longtemps was the soul of this house, even after he left it. From the moment he could walk and talk, anyone who lived here — as I did, when I was young — knew him like a brother."

A brother? A dead rebel soldier brother. I guess that would have seemed weirder to me before the train crash. A lot of things would.

"Or a son," she added in a whisper.

My mother moved through the shafts of moonlight, then stopped to run her fingers along the gash in the panel I had noticed earlier. "Ulysses was blessed with gifts unimaginable for a young man of his time. He was an engineer, a surgeon, a poet. And then came that horrible war. Ulysses was only twenty-four when he died. The war changed him forever."

I thought of Ronny and knew it was true. War did that.

Some part of me recognized noises in the house below. Shouting. A cry. Wood splintering.

"His soldiers gave his widow the poem he was writing when he died. It's the poem you have now, Derek."

"Okay . . ." I wanted to hear all this, but I didn't want to, either.

My mother looked closely at me. "Ulysses was there the first time the Rift opened."

I was stunned by her words. "What? *You* know about the Rift between the worlds?"

"All the Longtempses know about it," she said without emotion. "Ulysses was the one who discovered the opening between life and death. He called it the Wound. At the cost of his own life, he found a way to close it. That poem is the story of how Ulysses sent the dead back where they belong."

I nearly dropped to the floor.

"He . . . closed it?" I remembered what Ronny had been trying to say before. Was Ulysses Longtemps the "only person who ever . . ."?

"His young wife buried the poem with him," she went on. "The Longtemps widows after her pledged to keep it secret for as long as it took. The Widows' Pledge."

"For as long as it took?" I said. "For as long as *what* took?"

She turned her eyes to the palely lit windows. "For as long as it took for him to come back," she said simply.

What was she talking about?

"When I saw you had returned to Bayou

Malpierre," she continued, "I knew your journey to find your book had finally begun."

"You mean *his* book," I said. "And I'm not on any kind of journey. Unless you mean a journey away from the crazy dead people who are after me. This is insane —"

The shouting from the floors below was getting louder. Abby? Ronny? Or Erskine Cane?

My mother stepped closer. "You have to close the Wound again."

"What?"

"The evil you saw a hundred and fifty years ago is back. The Wound needs to be closed, just like you did the first time. That's why you're here."

I stared at her, wondering whether she had gone completely nuts over the last ten years. But something she said stirred in me. Bayou Malpierre. I hadn't smelled magnolias only at the cemetery before she abandoned me. I'd smelled them even before that.

At Bayou Malpierre, when I was four.

I had inhaled the scent of magnolias amid the rotting hulks of trees and vines the night I nearly drowned. I'd seen her face, her black hair loose in the water. I remembered it now. It felt like the fog in my head had suddenly cleared.

"You were there in the bayou, weren't you?" I said. "Ten years ago, the night I almost drowned?"

"And finally, we talk about it. Yes, Derek, I was there."

I felt as if hands were twisting my insides. The mystery of my life was going to be solved.

"You saved me that night!" I burst out. "Dad says it wasn't him. Ronny, too. Bonton Fouks didn't see who it was. No one knows anything. But your hair, I remember your hair in the water. And your perfume. It *was* you. You saved me, didn't you, Mom?"

"No, Derek," she said. "I didn't save you."

I saw the black hair coiling about her face in the water. I remembered my mother's fingers reaching for me, grasping my arms under the water.

"But you were there!" I said.

"I was there," she said, her lips trembling. "I saw you."

From the corner of my eye, I saw flames glimmer outside the window. I smelled wood burning, heard the clatter of sticks from the floors below. Abby yelling. Ronny gasping. The two of them calling my name.

"Derek!"

Mom saw the flames, too.

"Time is running out. You have to listen. Ulysses became an officer in the Louisiana Cavalry. He saw death up close, you'll remember it when you read those pages. One day his friend was slain in battle.

Ulysses held him in his arms, watched him die. Then later, he saw him return. Then another returned, and another. Ulysses discovered the Legion. He invented a way to send them back," she said, growing hoarse. "Do you understand? The Legion is growing. They want our world!"

I knew that. I'd been living it.

More glass shattered in the room just below us. Then came a heavy tread on the iron stairs, creaking with the weight.

"You wrote it all, step by step, Ulysses."

"I'm Derek, Mom," I said. "Derek —"

"Forget Derek now," she said firmly. "Ulysses, come out now. Your life depends on it. The Legion knows about you."

"Mom, stop it! Cut it out. You're talking crazy!" I was frozen. I could barely keep myself standing.

"Crazy?" she echoed. "Then how do you know the poem? The words that never left that book?"

"What — I don't — stop it!"

"Ulysses, come out now. Say good-bye to Derek. We have to stop the dead, like you did the first time. But your poem is like a code. Only you can under-stand your words —"

"Stop it!" I screamed. I didn't want to hear it. Couldn't.

She took my shoulders and shook me. "Ulysses, remember the bayou? Remember how you came back from the other side to help us? Remember!"

"Mom! Mom . . ." I wrenched myself free. "I don't care about him or his stupid words that you must have taught me. *You* saved me in the bayou. *You* saved me from drowning."

"I didn't save you. You drowned in the bayou that night."

I clutched her by the arms, pulled myself to her. "No, Mom! You saved me!"

"No, Derek . . . I killed you."

My legs buckled under me. I slipped from her and fell to the floor.

All at once — *foom-foom-foom!* — the walls shook. The door was battered from outside.

My mother pressed something into my hand, a tattered scrap of paper. I wanted to rip it up in front of her, but when I looked up there was only a flutter of curtains, and the whisper of a panel sliding back into place. She was gone.

"Mom? Mom! Don't leave me —"

The door splintered, and Abby tumbled in.

"The house is on fire!" she screamed. Her hands, strong and warm, took mine and pulled me out the door.

⊰ SIXTEEN ⊱

Deader Than Dead

"Cane is crazy trying to find you!" Abby said, leading me down the wobbling stairs. "He set the porch on fire, then the parlor —"

I shook my head to clear it. I finally understood who the Legion thought I was. The young captain. Captain Ulysses Perceval Longtemps. No. No. It was all wrong. It couldn't be. But I understood why they hadn't killed me before. They needed me to find the book. Now that I had, everything was simple.

Stop or be stopped.

Kill or be killed.

Cut or be cut.

It was a clear battle, and I was at the center of it. Nothing was by chance. Nothing had ever been by chance. I just didn't know it until now.

Clutching the book, I worked my way with Abby to the main stairs and the entrance hall, near the front doors of the house. Splintered wood was strewn everywhere. One-Arm charged into the room in front of five gray-faced soldiers.

"Surround them," he ordered.

They came at us, and Abby swung her cane so hard that it snapped over the one-armed conductor's head. He dropped to the floor, his head twisted garishly to the side. He shook wildly from waist to neck, a wisp of black fog unfurled from him, and he went still.

Abby screamed to see what she had done. The others paused for a moment, then rushed at us again.

I grabbed Abby's arm and pulled. "Out the back," I said, charging under the stairs. "Where's Ronny?"

"Escaped," she panted. "But I knew you were up there. I had to get you —"

Suddenly the pantry door burst off its hinges. There was Cane himself, torch blazing in his heavy hand. I saw in his eyes, his dead eyes, that he knew who I was, or was supposed to be — the young captain. Ulysses Longtemps.

Cane took a step. Without thinking, I ripped a picture frame off the wall and slammed it at his massive head. He simply held up his free hand and blocked it. The frame shattered. In that second, I ran into Cane's legs.

His feet slid together, sending his giant bulk

tumbling backward, but not before his fingers clawed like daggers across my forehead. They drew blood. I staggered out of the way, but only just. Cane's torch had set the banister ablaze.

"The back door!" Abby dragged me after her. But the back of the house thundered with feet. A troop of dead men swarmed out from under the stairs and pushed us toward the front of the house, which was already crackling with flames.

Waldo was with them. He was pointing at me.

With strength that came from who-knows-where, I swiveled on my heel and knocked blind, creepy little Waldo on his back like a bug. Then I grabbed Abby's hand and, shielding her face, pushed straight through the smoking front doors.

A wall of white flame met us on the other side. We were running so fast that we jumped straight through the fire and onto the steps, tumbling down to the garden.

When I got my bearings, I saw ten or fifteen trucks of all sizes rumbling across the fields with masses of translated souls standing in them. Among the trucks was the fire engine I'd seen before, now crawling with translated dead, some of them the police and firefighters who had come to rescue the living.

There must have been a few hundred Legion soldiers now.

All coming to stop me.

"Holy —" Abby gasped.

The front doors of the house burst open again, and Cane and the others stormed right through the flames at us, howling for blood. My blood.

But there was Ronny, plowing the old black hearse through the rows of marching dead. He roared over to us.

"Get in," he called, spinning out in the garden gravel.

Abby and I jumped into the car. Then Ronny peeled out, careening back through the columns of marching dead. Abby winced. But when I saw the Legion now, no matter how hideous, all I saw were numbers. I saw rows and rows of marching dead that needed to be stopped. Eliminated.

Was that what it meant to be a soldier in this horrible war?

Was I a soldier now?

Without warning, the rear window of the hearse shattered.

"Derek!" Abby gasped. "Behind you —"

Hands pulled me back into the coffin area. Missy Pudge loomed over me, her face gray and blubbery, eyes bulging. Translated. Sounds gargled in her throat, and her fists were like pistons, trying to wrench the book from me. Ronny skidded the hearse toward the stone bridge, picking up speed, while I ripped a curtain rope from the window and twisted it around Missy's gray face. She roared. Then she tore my hands away and threw me against the window. My head snapped on the glass, smashing my bad ear again. I kicked at the back door over and over until it swung wide.

Missy came at me again, but this time Abby thumped her in the face. The woman went flying out the back of the hearse and crumpled onto the dusty road.

"Thanks," I said to Abby, holding my ear. "I needed that."

"You're welcome," she panted. "And yes, you did."

Ronny slowed the hearse. "The Legion's taken the bridge. It's the only way out of here by car."

Through the trees, we could see that the old stone bridge was blocked by three trucks, unloading dozens of dead soldiers. We were cut off from the road on the far side.

Ronny jammed the hearse in reverse, fishtailed, and came to a stop. Masses of the dead were marching across the fields toward us.

We were trapped.

⊲ SEVENTEEN ⊳

The Cavalry

In the moment that followed, I heard the sound of distant hammering — or was it just the blood rushing in my wounded ear? It sounded like battering, thumping, pummeling wildly on iron horseshoes.

"Open the stables," someone said.

Abby turned to me. "What?"

Had *I* said it?

I turned to the misty garden and in my mind I saw the ghost officer and his wife take shape again. Captain Longtemps mounted his horse. But this time he set his face to the darkness and rode off. His call— *"Open the stables!"*

The air flashed to my left. A shriek pierced my ear, a hundred shrieks at once. Out of nowhere, like the storm of wind that threw us off the road earlier, now I saw the stable doors swing open and let loose the snorting and whinnying horses inside. One shape leaped from the mass of crumbled stone, then another and another, hooves clawing air, manes flying, all topped by soldiers in ragged uniforms of butter-nut and gray. It was his cavalry troop from a hundred and fifty years before — Ulysses's troop — their ghostly shapes leaping across the fields in the silver moonlight.

"Take back the bridge . . ." I whispered, and a cry rose up over the fields.

Take back the bridge!

Abby was still staring at me. "Derek? Derek . . ."

The long grass parted in front of the heaving ghost horses as they made for the bridge.

Ronny's eyes were fixed on the bridge. The trucks. The Legion. The screaming horses. "I see them. They're doing it."

"Who?" said Abby.

"Ghosts," said Ronny. "On horses."

"Are you serious?" Abby said. "You can both see them, but I can't? I mean, Ronny, sure. But you, Derek?"

I said nothing.

Like a tornado, the riders crashed across the fields, past the old slave quarters to the old stone bridge, and into the advancing Legion. The voices of the gray-faced dead were wild as they whirled on their feet, fell back. Sabers hacked across the air, sliced the moonlight into slivers of light and dark.

The dead massed closer, but the ghost riders,

though fewer, seemed to outnumber them ten to one. As if commanded, the horsemen swept around the Legion like an eerie and unstoppable storm. I shook. Abby gasped. Ronny murmured under his breath.

"Derek, what happened in that little room?" he asked.

I still said nothing.

Then Cane joined the fight, howling words into the night. The dead turned and moved back over the fields like water receding after a flood. Trucks started up one by one. The Legion retreated.

The bridge was open!

The chorus of shouts from the ghost riders grew louder, filled my ears until I could barely hear the evil dead as the cavalry pushed them across the fields. Away from us.

Away from me.

Soon, all that remained of the scene was what Ulysses never saw — his bride on her knees in the garden, her face in her hands, weeping. Weeping until she was suddenly no longer in white, but dressed head to toe in widows' weeds.

I knew that Ulysses's wife was the first of a long line of widows who pledged to keep his book safe.

Until it was needed. Until now.

Soon even the garden was empty.

Abby looked at me, tears in her eyes.

"Did you see her?" I asked.

She blinked away her tears and shook her head. "No. I was watching you."

I stared and stared as the ghost riders faded away across the fields, following Ulysses's orders.

My orders.

⊲ EIGHTEEN ⊳

The Boy Who...

Who was I to say there were no such things as ghosts?

Who was I to say the dead have no power over us?

Who *was* I?

As plumes of smoke filled the air and the red house burned, I told Ronny and Abby what the book was — a long poem, a way to heal the Rift, or the Wound, as I called it now. My mother had told me in the little room.

I told them the poem was written by . . . an ancestor of mine. I couldn't bring myself to say more.

Ronny placed his hand on my arm and spoke in a low voice. "Then we're done here. We have the book. The Legion will be back with a vengeance. But maybe we can find a way to do what Ulysses did. For now, we have to move. Let's go."

"One more thing," I said, wringing my arm free and climbing out of the hearse.

"Derek —" Abby said.

"One more thing!" I repeated, stepping away.

I dug into my pocket, fishing for the paper my mother had given me. I unfolded it slowly and read it by the glow of the burning house.

Dear Derek, it began.

I turned it over and over in my mind — my name of fourteen years. I loved imagining the sound of her voice speaking it.

Dear Derek . . . Dear Derek . . .

I hoped that, in the words that followed, she would take back everything she had told me in the little room. Maybe it was all a test, a dream, a lie.

You will hate me for what I have done. But you will see I had no choice. Ulysses was our only hope then, and our only hope now. I gave up my youngest son so that Ulysses could come back — in you — to fight again. Derek, poor little Derek. He died in the bayou that night. He died. Soon you will remember how you went into my little boy.

I crumpled the letter in rage. "I won't believe it! I won't!" I fell to my knees.

"Derek!" said Abby, climbing out of the hearse and running over to me.

"No!" I stood and moved away from her. From inside my head I heard the reply — cold, clear, and final.

You must believe it.

Suddenly, I was back in the bayou on that night so long ago. I saw my mother's hands in the water above me, not grasping for me as I had thought, and the face of the young man, Ulysses, moving toward me through the water. And I became the water . . . I became . . . him.

Safeguard your book with your life. Lose it, and we lose the war. Decipher it, follow its directions, and the Legion will fall, the Wound will be closed, and life can return. Not for you, but for the others.

Shaking, I looked across the fields and saw only darkness. What was I supposed to do? Would I rot like Ronny? Why could I bleed, when he couldn't? What was the difference between us?

My future was in the past. How did the dead move forward? The answer was in the last paragraph.

I began this letter addressing you by my son's name, Derek Longtemps Stone. I close it by calling you your rightful name.

Go forth, Ulysses Perceval Longtemps. Take up your journey of so many years ago, the voyage only you know — the road of ghosts. The hope of the whole world goes with you.

Your great-granddaughter. Your mother.

Louise Pearline Longtemps

My legs couldn't hold me up. I collapsed to the ground, crushing the letter in my fist. Abby tried to still my shaking hands, but hers were trembling, too.

"What does it say?"

"Let us read it," said Ronny, walking up behind me.

"No," I said. "It's nothing. Nothing." I shoved the letter into my pocket. I couldn't admit it. Not to others. Not to myself. Not yet.

A hot wind shrieked past the burning house, fanning the flames.

Ronny turned to me. "Keep your secret for now. At least you found what the key was hiding before they did. A storm's coming. We'll hide tonight, then decide what to do in the morning. The Legion will be after us in even greater numbers now."

My mother had said the same thing.

The Legion is growing. They want our world!

And Abby's mother — the messenger — had told me, "Find the First. One day only!"

But if I was the captain — if — if I had closed the Wound once before, maybe I could do it again. Maybe I could. Me.

And you?

Do you think this lets you off the hook?

Don't think that just because we held them off this once, you can go back to your iPods and your malls and your cookouts and your normal life.

I can tell you right now, this war won't let you.

The Legion won't let you.

So what should you do?

Run.

Another hot wind swept past. Amaranthia, the great red house, had waited a hundred and fifty years for Ulysses Perceval Longtemps to return. Now it shuddered and quivered and finally collapsed on itself.

Amaranthia. Lost again.

I thought back to that morning, only nine hours before. If I believed what my mother had told me, it was now so far in the past it meant nothing.

That was the past of Derek Stone.

The boy who died.

"Ronny's right," said Abby, tugging my arm gently.

"My mother's out there somewhere. Maybe she'll help us again. There's nothing for us here. We have to go. Our job's not done yet."

It hurt to see Abby becoming a soldier, too. Like Ronny. And like me.

Some army we had.

Maybe we stood a chance.

With a last look at the burning wreckage, I climbed back into the hearse, turning toward the voyage only I knew — the road of ghosts.

Ronny started the engine, threw the old hearse in gear, and we raced off into the gathering night.

THE GHOST ROAD

To Those Who Can't Remain

⊰ ONE ⊱

Wild Hearses

After I finished throwing up, we started driving again.

My brother — Ronny — and Abby Donner were silent and tired as we tore up the foggy roads outside Coushatta. We'd been driving all night, and it was the third time I'd gotten sick in as many hours.

"Sorry," I mumbled, as I had the first two times. But I wasn't. Throwing up was my body's way of saying, "Nope. Can't digest this insanity. No way."

You'd chuck it all up too if, right out of the blue, someone told you — no, *hundreds* of people told you —

"You hear that?" Abby interrupted my thoughts.

Ronny tore his eyes from the rearview mirror and slowed the hearse. "What?"

"Shhh." I turned and looked out the back window. "I hear it, too. . . ."

Ronny pulled to the shoulder of the road near a stretch of weedy fence, flicked off the headlights, and cocked his head. "I don't hear anything. You guys are —"

Abby screamed, "A truck!"

Wrong. Three trucks, racing out of the fog behind us.

Ronny jammed his foot on the gas and spun the wheel. The hearse slid behind the fence, throwing me and Abby to the floor. Ronny jerked to a stop as the trucks shot past us, racing north toward Shreveport.

I couldn't see the faces of the drivers, but I could hear their voices — whining, angry, squealing, groaning. I knew who they were.

Dead men.

The trucks didn't slow down, just barreled up the road and out of sight. We had escaped. For now.

Ronny snorted. "Well, that could've been bad."

Abby climbed back into her seat and swatted him with the road map. She wasn't being playful. "Jerk! I don't want to rebreak my ankle! Why can't you just drive like a normal person?"

Ronny turned to her, his face suddenly cold. "You want reasons?"

That was a joke. Sort of.

Ronny wasn't a normal person. He was as dead as the men in those trucks.

That probably explained why he wasn't a great driver. But with the Legion after you, bad driving isn't such a big deal.

The Legion?

Man, I hope you've been listening to what I've already told you, because there's not much time for a big story.

Today it would all happen.

Ronny skidded the car — a beat-up 1954 Cadillac hearse about a block and a half long — back onto the road, and we drove on.

To start from the beginning, my name is Derek Stone. More about me later. What you really need to know now is that Ronny died a few weeks back in a train wreck. It happened at a place called Bordelon Gap on the Red River.

Abby and I were there, too. I was injured and Abby was in a coma for a month, but we're okay — more or less. Not Ronny. He was one of nine people who died. But he came back a few weeks later. In fact, all the crash victims came back, including my father and Abby's mother, Madeline Donner. None of them were themselves anymore, except maybe my dad. I wasn't sure about him.

How did they come back from the dead?

Through a thing called the Rift — or the

Wound — a tear in the fabric between this world and the next. The opening allowed dead souls to reanimate dying bodies, if the manner of death was the same. That's called translation.

Turns out — surprise! — the road to the afterlife is a two-way street.

Most of the victims were now inhabited by the souls of convicts who had died in an almost identical train crash at the same place in 1938. Except for Ronny, Abby's mom, and maybe my dad, the souls that returned were the advance troops of a huge dead army. The Legion.

The Legion's mission was simple: to bring their dead comrades back in huge numbers, to flood the land with evil, to destroy the living, and to spread their world of death here.

Not much. Just that.

Why do they want to come back? Ronny told me the land of the dead is a harsh place for evil souls — a world of perpetual torture. So over the centuries they banded together to fight the good souls. It's kind of like revenge. They want out of the afterlife.

They want to be back here.

Right now, the Legion's troops were driving north under the command of a guy named Erskine Cane. He was a murderer and arsonist, now in the body of a soldier. After translations at Bayou Malpierre (a creepy place where I nearly drowned when I was four) and Amaranthia (my mother's broken-down family home), the evil dead now numbered about two hundred fifty.

Translation is a really ugly thing. It's horrible, the way the dead soul forces its way into a dying body. A good soul would never translate unless it were absolutely necessary, unless there were no choice.

But the evil dead have lost whatever makes others good. So, they want to come back? They translate.

Erskine Cane had been calling the shots so far, but I knew that the Legion's overall leader was someone even more powerful. He was known only as the First, and he was planning something huge. My guess was that he was going to blast the Wound wide open.

And he was going to do it today.

How did I know that?

According to Abby's dead mother, my job was to find the First, and I had "one day only."

She told me that yesterday.

Nothing like running out of time to add some pressure.

"Ronny, will you slow down!" Abby burst out.

"Uh, no," he said. "It'll be dawn in an hour, and I'm pretty sure it was your dead mom who said —"

"Don't talk about her like that!" Abby shouted.

"Stuff it, and find a better road map," Ronny replied.

Yeah. They weren't getting along. Ronny was on edge like nobody's business. I knew one reason. He had a patch of gray flesh on his neck and chin that had been spreading by the hour.

He was decaying fast.

I'm still learning the rules, but I'm pretty sure it was happening because Ronny had been translated on land. I'd seen enough dead people by now to know that bodies translated in water weren't decaying as quickly. That was because the Wound was located in water — the Red River, to be exact, which bends across Louisiana from one corner to the other. Dead souls moved through the river from the Wound, then translated into the dying wherever they found them.

I'd discovered some of this in old books, some on the Internet, and some from the crazy people I'd met over the last few days.

Ronny told me a lot, too. The soul that returned in his body was a farm boy named Virgil Black, who had died in the 1938 crash. For seventy years, Virgil had been a soldier fighting the Legion in the after-life. He was one of the good guys. Now that the Legion was here, I was glad to have him on my side.

"Derek, hurry up and read that thing," Ronny said. "We don't have forever."

"Cut Derek some slack, will you?" said Abby.

"Just read it!"

Right. The voices of the dead weren't the only things crowding my brain. There was *The Ghost Road*, a fifty-page poem I'd discovered at Amaranthia. It had been scribbled in scratchy black ink during the Civil War by a young captain named Ulysses Longtemps.

He's . . . an ancestor of mine.

The poem describes how Ulysses witnessed the First's translation during Louisiana's Red River Campaign in 1864. Ulysses then discovered the Wound between our worlds and closed it. My mother told me that I was supposed to follow the poem, discover the Wound like he did, and seal it shut again.

Terrific. I didn't like poems, did everything I could not to read them in school, and here I had to read a very long one in order to save the world.

My mother also said *The Ghost Road* was written in a kind of code — one that only I could understand. It's like Waldo Fouks, that creepy boy I met in the bayou, told me: I'm special.

It was a poem and it was written in code. Two big strikes against it, in my opinion.

Or maybe three. The poem wasn't even complete. I'd flipped to the end only to discover that the poem stopped abruptly in the middle of a line. Of course it did. Ulysses had died before he could finish it.

I'd found the book a few hours ago, but I'd barely had a chance to read it, never mind try to understand it. But holding it in my hands was like holding a living thing, somehow. Like cradling a beating heart.

Ronny swung his head around. "Anything?"

"I'm still looking," I said.

"Look faster."

When I opened to the first page of the poem, I saw the title inked in slanting black letters. A slash of rusty red ran from the bottom left corner to the upper right corner. It was a single stripe of color, a stain, blood soaked into the fibers of the page. It had become part of the poem it had seeped into.

I thought of the phrase "written in blood."

Whatever *The Ghost Road* was, the Legion wanted it. They wanted me, I knew. But they also wanted that book — wrinkled pages, bloodstain, and all.

Ronny slowed the hearse as we came to a crossroads. A lone stop sign was stuck in the ground, tilted severely away from the road. It looked like someone had crashed into it.

Ronny snickered. "Okay, now what?"

"Derek, can you read the words again?" Abby asked, scanning the map by the dim dashboard light.

It was dark in the car, but I found the lines of the poem that seemed to describe the place we were looking for. I read them aloud.

"'The river bends like weeping willow limbs
And there I thought I saw a widow bend to her dead
love,
And saw his body bending in the tangled swamp.'"

"Lots of bending going on," said Ronny coolly.

I didn't read them the next line, though I couldn't get it out of my mind.

By end of day, I knew that dead love might be me.

"There's a place called Cemetery Bend coming up in a few miles," said Abby, tracing her finger across the map. "It's on the river, and there's a cross marked here. Do you think —"

"More than you do," Ronny cut in. The engine growled as he raced off again, burning rubber.

Abby sulked. "You waste gas every time you do that."

"So do you, when you open your mouth," Ronny muttered.

"Well, at least *I'm* not decaying," Abby said.

"Shut up!" I cried. "And pull over!"

Ronny braked fast, and I jumped out of the car, feeling my stomach flip over again. But it wasn't their arguing that was making me sick.

In Ulysses Longtemps's old room at Amaranthia,

among a chorus of weeping widows and the smell of magnolia, my mother had told me a terrible secret.

Leaning away from the hearse, spilling what was left of my guts onto the ground, I remembered every word and wondered what kind of hearse had carried me when I had died.

⊰ TWO ⊱

Hello-I-Must-Be-Going

When I had died.

If I actually believed what my mother told me in that dusty room at Amaranthia, I hadn't *nearly* drowned in that filthy bayou when I was four. I'd just plain drowned.

Not only that, but at the instant I drowned, I was translated.

That's right.

I was reanimated by the soul of the old poet captain, Ulysses Longtemps. Why? Because the world needed him more than me. After all, I was no one, but Ulysses Longtemps had closed the Wound.

In other words, since I was four I haven't been quite myself. I've been him.

It's like this:

Hi, I'm Derek Stone. I've been dead most of my life.

Or this:

Hi, I'm Derek. My next birthday is a hundred and fifty years ago.

You can't imagine the mess in my head right now. Derek Stone. Ulysses Longtemps. Old ghosts. The evil Legion.

Everyone trying to get a word in.

Abby didn't know about it yet. Poor Abby. Just a nice girl holding a cheesecake when I first saw her on that train. It seemed like a hundred lifetimes ago. Ronny didn't know who I really was, either, but I wondered how long it would take him to guess. He was a fellow dead guy, after all.

I hadn't figured out how to tell them. I couldn't believe it myself.

Except that I'd looked at it from every angle I could think of, and my being dead was the only thing that made sense. I saw dead people. I heard their voices. I could chat with ghosts. I understood things about Ulysses Longtemps that I couldn't possibly have known otherwise. I'd remembered bits of his poem long before I had ever seen that old book.

"Here." Abby handed me a paper towel through the car window.

I wiped my mouth and got back in.

Trees flashed by. Abby murmured something about the map. Ronny muttered behind the wheel and kept driving.

I knew that it was up to me to find Cemetery Bend and the Wound between life and death.

Ulysses had translated into me for that exact reason. As my mother had told me: *Safeguard your book with your life. Lose it, and we lose the war. Decipher it, follow its directions, and the Legion will fall, the Wound will be closed, and life can return.*

I only had one day to close the Wound, and if I couldn't follow the directions in the poem, things would get really nasty — really quickly. Ulysses' poem said:

> *. . . dark souls will flood the darkened earth from every drop of dark water . . .*

Lots of darkness going on.

"I thought you guys could hear the dead," Abby said, her eyes fixed on the rearview mirror. "The Legion's back!"

I swiveled in my seat and looked back at the curving road.

Headlights glowed in the fog behind us. I counted four distinct pairs of lights, but there were probably more. The drivers' screeching echoed in my ears now. I'd been so wrapped up in my thoughts that I hadn't heard the dead. But Ronny hadn't heard them, either. Why not?

"Lose them," I said.

Ronny scoffed. "This is what I was born for!"

That was true. Virgil Black used to race tractors back in Shongaloo when he was alive.

Ronny slammed his foot on the gas, and we pulled ahead. The voices of the dead shrieked in my bad ear, and the trucks didn't hang back. The front one sped up so quickly it rammed our bumper.

Tires screeched as Ronny slid the car around a corner, scraping the guardrail. Sparks flew. He righted the wheel and roared straight ahead. He was good.

A police siren wailed, and a cruiser tore out suddenly from a side road. A motorcycle cop drove right behind the cruiser. The tinny loudspeaker demanded that we pull over.

Ronny sped up.

If the Legion had been smart, or if they had cared, they would have split up and gone on their way. But they weren't smart. They were deadly. And the only things they cared about were getting that book and getting rid of me.

Whoever I was.

As we raced along a stretch of rain-flooded road, I saw the first truck behind us slow down to let the motorcycle and cruiser pull closer. As they did, the truck driver braked suddenly. The motorcycle rear-ended the truck, sending its driver flying into the woods by the side of the road. A second truck tore out of the fog and rammed the police car into the back of the first truck. It was sandwiched. Two other trucks pulled up around it and shrieked to a stop.

I wanted to look away — but I couldn't. Through the back window, I saw dead men throw the cruiser doors open and descend on the police, rolling them onto the flooded shoulder.

"No," I said. "Another translation?"

"Are we just going to leave —" Abby started.

"You can stay," said Ronny. "I'm getting out of here!"

We raced up the road, and fog surrounded us again. I turned in my seat and stared blankly out the front window of the hearse. No use looking back now. The cops were goners.

"Those poor men," said Abby quietly.

"Better them than us," said Ronny. "Read the map."

Abby shook her head but said nothing.

There was nothing to say. Death surrounded us. All we could do was keep it from getting too close.

Then it surrounded us for real.

Something flashed by the window on my right. It matched the speed of the hearse, even as we went faster. I edged my eyes toward it, not wanting to see. A face — white — dead, flying through the fog outside the car.

I turned away. "No. Please."

"What?" asked Abby, turning in her seat to look at me.

I shut my eyes tight. When I opened them, I saw a

second face speeding through the fog on the other side of the hearse. It spoke.

We're ready. Lead us.

"No . . ."

The first face repeated it. *We're ready!*

I glanced at Ronny in the rearview mirror. His eyes were set on the road ahead.

Why didn't he hear the voices or see the faces? What was wrong with him? If he was dead, like me, why couldn't he hear the ghosts? He always used to!

Suddenly, they were in the backseat with me.

Two ghosts in old uniforms — the Rebel uniforms I had seen on the ghosts at Amaranthia. They had ashen skin, hard black eyes. They pointed out the window to my right.

There . . . there!

"What? Right?" I said. "Turn right?"

The ghosts wailed. *There!*

"Turn right!" I cried.

"Are you kidding?" said Ronny. "It's just woods."

"We're still three miles from Cemetery Bend," Abby added.

"Turn! Now!" I shouted.

Ronny jerked the wheel fast. The ghosts vanished with a shriek as we bounced off the road and into the woods.

"Ronny, slow down!" Abby shouted.

I hit the ceiling and crumpled back down to the seat. Abby fell to the floor again. We struck a stump. I heard the rear bumper rip off. We banged and nicked trees one after another until a bright light burst through the branches and blinded us.

"What —" Ronny cried. He slammed on the brakes.

A man jumped out of the trees in front of us, holding a musket. "Halt!"

I screamed.

⊲| THREE |⊳

Night Work

"Stop screaming!" Ronny spat as the hearse slid to a stop on the pine needles. "What are you, two years old?"

When he shut off the engine, it was eerily quiet. The fierce light vanished. A musty smell suddenly seeped through the windows.

"Y'all okay in there?"

Leaning toward the car was a late-middle-aged man with fat rosy cheeks, a squat hat pulled low over his forehead, and a beard like a shag rug hanging from ear to ear. He looked like an out-of-work Santa — except that he wore a uniform of filthy mustard-colored wool and carried an old musket.

"Y'all okay?" he repeated, squinting into the car.

Abby drew in a quick breath. "Did we, like, take a wrong turn and come out a hundred years ago?"

Santa laughed. "A hundred and forty-four! This is April of 1864. You musta gotten the e-mail!"

Great. Just what we needed — more crazy.

"Another hour and you would have missed the big battle," he added.

"Battle?" Ronny said. "Between who?"

"Depends," Santa said, leaning on the car. "You a Mouton or a Taylor? Taylors are right about here. Mouton's men are gathering west of Swamp Road." He paused to chuckle. "They call it Swamp Road on account of some days it's one, some days it's the other. Wagons are coming soon, if you want to hitch a ride. Beauchamp's men haven't arrived at all yet."

Ronny turned to us. "Who's crazy here, him or me?"

I couldn't process it, either, until I remembered that Taylor, Beauchamp, and Mouton were names of Confederate commanders during the Civil War.

"Wait a second," I said. "Is there going to be a . . ." I couldn't think of the word. "A . . . reenactment of a battle?"

"Why, yessir!" Santa said, eyeing Ronny's darkening neck and scratching his own. "Largest gathering of what we call 'living historians' ever. Five thousand soldiers, fifteen hundred horses, a thousand wagons. Starts this morning at dawn."

The man couldn't seem to come up with a complete sentence.

Abby turned to me. "Why didn't we know about this?"

"Maybe we've been a little out of touch?" I said, climbing out of the hearse.

I glanced around and realized that my heart was pounding like a hammer on an anvil. I had never been there before . . . right?

We were completely surrounded by woods, but I somehow knew what lay beyond them — undulating hillocks and channels, all bunched up here and there like a wrinkled carpet. There was a long field, sloping downward from the road to the river. Thick woods bordered it on either side, along with sodden ditches, swamps, stone walls, and rocky outcroppings. A nightmare of a battlefield. And I knew every inch of it.

'Twas there we massed, that swamp upon a swamp . . .

"Is this Cemetery Bend?" I asked no one in particular.

"Abba-solutely, son," said Santa, flicking his eyes to the sky. The guy liked to talk. "Skirmish at the crest of Bloody Meadow comes at first light, 'bout an hour. You'll need to get your car out of here. We're in 1864, remember."

I *did* remember. It was almost like reading the lines right off the page.

. . . blue-clad invaders drove their wagons up the road,
While graybacks we, we massed our steeds,
Our thoughts all haunted by what lay ahead.

My heart sank. I didn't know exactly what lay ahead, but I was sure none of it was going to be good.

The bright light flashed over us again.

"What *is* that?" Abby asked, climbing out of the car and standing next to me. Ronny stayed put behind the wheel.

Santa moved a few paces away, then cleared his throat and swung his musket out toward the woods. As the light moved on, we could see what looked like a big river barge just off the nearest bank. It was a flatboat with a large cabin at one end. Cranes and shovels were digging at the water from the flat part of the barge.

"Night work on the river," the pretend soldier said. "That there is a dredger. Deepens the river at this point every ten years or so. River clogs with silt and dirt. Dredgers drag it out from Shreveport all the way down to Bordelon, where it gets too narrow."

The name rushed through my veins like ice. Bordelon. Where our train had crashed. Where Ronny had been translated. Where I had begun to hear the dead.

"Dicky Meade owns the dredger. He promised to go quiet for the reenactment," Santa continued. "Battle ends with fireworks from his boat at dusk. His boat's gonna be our teakettle!"

That sparked something in me.

While silent pass the teakettles, breathing steam and rage,

The phantom comes, the phantom goes.

Talk about code. The phantom?

"Teakettle?" said Abby. "Um . . . what?"

Two men in similar dirty uniforms joined the first one. They glanced up and down the length of our hearse and grinned, each showing a set of yellow teeth.

One of the men sighed. "You folks need to be educated. A teakettle's a ship! Federal ironclad, with iron plates on the outside. Teakettle. Get it?"

Ronny drummed his fingers loudly on the steering wheel. "Are we done here?"

"No," I said, turning back to the reenactors. "Tell me about the teakettles."

Santa looked delighted to "educate" the city folk.

"The big kettle in the campaign was a Union gunboat called the *Eastport*," he said. "The captain scuttled it — sank it — rather than let it fall into Rebel hands. Because it was a munitions boat, it blew up something fierce, and kept exploding under the water. Flooded the banks of Cemetery Bend during the battle, all the way up to Swamp Road. There'll be fireworks at dusk, meant to represent the scuttling of the *Eastport*. Dicky Meade is pulling out all the stops —"

Before he could finish, the sky opened up.

"Dang!" said Santa, hunching his shoulders and turning his face up to the rain. "Now we're gonna be mud fighting. And here come the wagons —"

Abby and I jumped back into the car. From my half-open window, I smelled horses. The squeal of wooden wheels and the shouting of men echoed nearby.

Rain pooled quickly in the grass and on the old road behind us. Within minutes, it was a torrent, coming cold and heavy. Men lurched among the trees in bunches, all calling and yelling.

"Cemetery Bend is already a swamp," Santa barked through the car window, shielding his face with his arm. "In this rain, there could be lots of friendly fire. Thank goodness these guns don't actually shoot. Five thousand come to battle, five thousand fight, and five thousand go home safe and sound!"

Abby turned to me. I knew we were thinking the same thing. Five thousand might come and fight, but they wouldn't all go home safe and sound.

The Legion was coming.

Still, was there something else about the teakettle and the fireworks? Something had clicked in my brain. I just wasn't sure what. Santa said that the

Eastport was a munitions boat that had exploded under the water.

Was that how the Wound had opened in the first place?

I suddenly felt dumb. Why couldn't I understand anything? Thanks to the ghosts, we had found Cemetery Bend. But now what? Time was running out. I had to decipher the code.

"Back your hearse to Swamp Road," Santa yelled through the downpour, pointing his musket the way we'd come. "There's parking in the far field." He turned and hustled off with the yellow-teeth men.

We rolled the windows closed.

"Men didn't play with guns in my day," Ronny muttered.

"Should we tell them we think something's going to happen?" asked Abby. "The Legion and everything?"

"They would never believe it," said Ronny. "But you can bet this battlefield is where it will happen, so it's where we need to be. You stay here. I'll park the car and be back."

I felt hopelessness almost crush me as Abby and I stepped out into the rain. The reenactment *was* the perfect cover for a mass translation. Five thousand men — fresh bodies — at the site of a battle on the Red River.

But how would it happen?

How could we get anyone to believe us?

And how could we possibly stop it?

⊰ FOUR ⊱

Flooded Ditches

Abby and I followed a small group of "soldiers" to a campfire in the woods.

Some men huddled under cloaks. Some stood under trees, laughing, their uniforms already soaked through. "Realistic!" I heard one say.

He was right. It had rained during the original battle of Cemetery Bend, too. I can't say how I knew that.

About a dozen men crouched around the hissing fire, including Santa and his yellow-teeth friends. They had hung a canvas sheet between some trees to protect them from the drenching rain. The shelter collected smoke, but the men didn't seem to mind. They flapped the edge of the canvas, inviting us in, and Abby scampered underneath.

"Maybe today's not a good day for a battle," Abby said to the men, giving me a look.

"Because of the rain?" one of the yellow-teeth guys scoffed. "Rain don't stop soldiers."

"But it makes everything more dangerous," I put in. "People could die today. I mean for real."

The yellow-teeth men both looked at me at the same time. It was almost like they were connected. "What exactly are you trying to say, son?" one of them asked while the other scratched his head.

How to answer?

I took the plunge. What was the worst that could happen?

"The dead are coming. Hundreds of them —"

"Wooo-hooo!" said the other yellow-teeth man, grinning. "You got some kind of screw loose." He turned to Abby. "See to your boyfriend, miss. He's crazy!"

"He's not . . . my boyfriend," Abby said. I thought she might be blushing.

"You saying he *is* crazy, then?" Santa said.

The soldiers laughed.

Yeah, hilarious.

"Derek, just let it go," Abby whispered. "Let's wait for Ronny."

She was right. The whole dead-coming-back thing sounded insane when you just came out with it; I knew that. I was about to sit down next to Abby when I spotted a reenactor standing in the rain a few feet away. He wasn't much older than Ronny, and he was so thin that I almost hadn't seen him at all.

"Hey," I called.

His eyes flicked toward me, then away. His hair — blond, filthy, soaked, and matted — stuck out below the edges of his cap. He held a pistol in one hand, its barrel pointing to the ground. His legs were bowed, as if he had grown up riding horses. His boots were torn and ragged, and his trousers were ripped. I had to admit that it was an authentic look for a young kid.

"Come under the tent," I said. "There's room —"

Abby looked up at me. So did three of the men around the fire.

"You'll be leaving us soon," the young soldier said to me.

I shrugged. "Maybe."

What difference did that make?

"Maybe what?" Santa asked.

"Maybe we'll be leaving," I said.

"No problem," one of the yellow-teeth men said. "There's still an hour before dawn. Reporters just left. You might have a bit of trouble getting past the police cordon, though. Because of the rain, the fields are sure to flood. They'll want to keep civilians back behind the line."

"You'll be leaving soon," the boy said again.

"What's your name?" I asked him.

"Frank," an older guy crouching next to the fire responded. He looked up at me. But I wasn't talking to him.

"Jeremiah Ross," said the boy, still looking away. His voice was faint, maybe from yelling. "Folks call me Jem. You know that. Or maybe you forgot. Time on the battlefield does things to your head."

That made me think he had actually fought in a real battle, not just weekend reenactments.

"Okay . . . ," I said softly, stepping toward him. I was getting rained on, but I didn't care.

Abby rose. "Derek?"

"You start seeing things," the young man continued. "Can't sleep, can't sit, can't stand, your head aches, your heart aches from dawn to dark to dawn again until heat rips your side, and you fall, and there is only gray. . . ."

He drifted off. His words were beautiful, but nutty. It seemed like he was in some kind of trance.

"But if it's not fun, why do you do it?" I said to him.

"Oh, it's fun," Frank piped up. "It's plenty fun. A weekend away from the wives! Get under the tarp, kid." He gestured to me.

"Fun?" Jem replied. "I saw my brother take a musket shot to the neck. Died in a ditch. They all died in ditches." He shrugged and spat on the ground.

"Sorry," I said, flinching. I paused for a minute. "Why don't you come under the tent?"

"Who?" Frank asked.

"Derek?" Abby whispered. "Are you okay?"

I stared at Jem. "Come on under the tent."

"No. I've got to show you some things." He finally turned his face to the firelight.

Half of it wasn't there. Jem's right cheek and half his lips were gone.

I must have made a noise.

"Derek?" said Abby, walking out into the rain and putting her hand on my arm. She nearly stepped on the boy's foot.

Jem squinted at her. "That girl shouldn't be here. This is going to get ugly."

"Derek, are you all right?" Abby asked.

"Captain, come with me," said Jem.

That's when I knew.

No one saw the young soldier but me.

⊰ FIVE ⊱

From the Tower

As soon as I realized Jem was a ghost, I could see the obvious signs that I'd missed. Rain was pouring right through him, splashing on the ground below as if he wasn't there at all.

"I've got to show you some things," he repeated.

His eyes were black marbles, boring into mine. He didn't blink at all. Then he walked off through the rain. I glanced back at Abby and saw Ronny picking through the woods toward us. I turned away from them.

"Derek, wait," Abby said.

I didn't.

"Ronny, hurry," Abby called. "Derek's seeing someone."

Frank hooted. "Must make you jealous!"

Jem was already deep in the trees. I ran after him.

In a clearing ahead stood a tall, square rough-log structure — an observation tower. The top, which was fifty or so feet high, was a roofed and railed platform above the treetops. Wooden stairs zig-zagged from the base up.

Without pausing to look for me, Jem stumbled onto the stairs and began to climb. I was out of breath by the time I reached the top. You'd think I'd have been in better shape after all the running from the dead I'd been doing.

In the corner of the platform, a short kid about the same age as Ronny was sitting on a little stool made of logs. He wore a park uniform shirt and a name tag that said *Chad*. He flicked his eyes up from his iPod when I got up there.

He sighed and stood. "Ooh, a visitor. Lucky me. So the rain didn't keep you away, like every-one else?"

Of course, the kid didn't see Jem there with us.

Sighing to himself, Chad popped one earbud out and launched into his little memorized speech.

"Welcome to the official observation post of the Cemetery Bend Memorial Battlefield. I'm one of sev-eral guides you may meet during today's reenactment. This tower was erected in 1964 on the hundredth anniversary of the Civil War Battle of Cemetery Bend. It also acts as a bell tower for official battle-field events. You'll hear the bell ring in a little while."

He motioned mechanically to a thick rope that hung from the top of the roof and passed through a hole in the floor to the ground.

The guy droned on, bored by his own words. Chad reminded me of how Ronny used to be, before he died.

As I only half-listened, I got my first good look at the battlefield through the mist and smoke. It was several square miles, centered on Bloody Meadow, a wrinkled landscape of channels and bumps that were riddled with flooding ditches. The meadow bent first one way, then another, from Swamp Road all the way down to the riverbank.

I saw the gray stones of a cemetery in the woods below. A little distance away was a long, low building, like a stable. On the near side of the meadow, between the tower and the cemetery, stood a big barn. It leaned away from the wagon path, like it might topple at any minute.

It was hard to look at the field without feeling like I knew it. *Really* knew it. In my mind I saw men charging across the meadow from different angles, heard their shouts mix with the blasts of weapons. Two and a half thousand had died before the Battle of Cemetery Bend was over.

"The foot of Bloody Meadow," Jem said to me,

pointing to where the rutted field met the river. "Too many died there. That's where Beauchamp's Butchers were killed."

"What?" I said.

Chad stopped his spiel. "*What* what?" He looked at me impatiently.

"Beauchamp's Butchers," I said.

"Butchers?" another voice chimed in. Ronny had reached the top of the tower. He wasn't nearly as out of breath as I'd been. "Sounds about right. What did they do?"

The guide didn't seem interested in Ronny's appearance. He riffled lazily through his brochure. "There's not much here. I remember people saying that Clarence Beauchamp was a nutcase, but had, like, this loyalty thing with his troops. He went berserk on the battlefield, killing civilians — anyone he thought was helping the Yankees take Cemetery Bend."

Jem's eyes drifted to the riverbank at the foot of the meadow. "The other troops pushed them into the river after they mutinied at the height of the battle. A massacre, some say."

"What happened to Beauchamp?" I asked.

"Some other general led his troops against Beauchamp's. Finally had to kill them all. In the water. It's what ended the battle." Chad's eyes widened. It was the first time he'd looked anything but indifferent. "They say their ghosts still haunt the cemetery. A couple thousand creepy killers. It was insane, dude."

Abby finally appeared and leaned on the railing, slowly rotating her ankle. "Sorry. It still hurts."

Jem shook his head. "She shouldn't be here."

"You're s-s-seeing somebody, aren't you?" Ronny whispered to me. "But I can't. How is th-th-that possible?"

Was Ronny stuttering now? Or was it just the cold rain? I tried to ignore it and turned back to Chad. "People are going to die here today. You should go home."

He laughed. "Not me. I get paid by the hour. Plus, the rain is keeping most tourists away. No prob for me. I still get paid."

"Ask him about that thing," Jem said, nodding toward the dredging barge.

I did. The guide peered toward the river.

"I don't know," he said. "Hold on." He shuffled noisily through his brochure again, clearly annoyed at having to do what he was getting paid for.

"The dredging started ten years ago, when I was, like, seven," he said absentmindedly. "In Shreveport, then on south. Here it is." He read from the brochure. "'Arriving at this part of the river a decade ago, the dredging company discovered massive ledges of bedrock beneath the accumulated silt. They realized that in order to increase the underwater area, they would have to detonate explosives in the river bed. A series of powerful explosions disturbed enough of the bedrock to effectively deepen the river.'"

"Ten y-years ago?" said Ronny, giving me the eye. "Not exactly a surprise, is it?"

My mind raced. If the Wound was somewhere in the riverbed, had it first opened when the *Eastport* was destroyed in 1864? And had it opened again when the bedrock was detonated ten years ago to dredge the river? Could the two explosions have been so sudden and so massive that they'd ripped the veil?

I looked out at the dredger, which was nearly motionless in the river.

I knew, of course, that the afterlife wasn't exactly a geographic location. It wasn't that simple or that physical. But the separation between us and the afterlife must have been something, after all. A kind of veil between the living world and the land of the dead that you couldn't see or feel but was still there.

It reminded me of a passage from a book I'd read when this whole thing began. *Afterlives* by Tomas Deak had convinced me that translation was possible.

A ghost is a mere shadow, like the shadow cast from a distant object. That shadow can be seen in our world from time to time — as in a "haunting." But the distant object from which it is cast is its soul. After death, the soul resides exclusively in the afterlife — unless it returns in physical form.

I knew that. Ghosts pass through the veil all the time without there being an actual hole. But the Wound was different. It must be where the veil between the worlds was weakest. It was something like a rip, a tear, but so small that only one soul could pass through it at a time. *Afterlives* went on:

. . . it is speculated that when the veil between the worlds of life and death breaks open — a sort of rip in the fabric — souls may be able to transport into dying bodies if the manner of death is the same. The more similar the manner of death, the better the fit.

That would explain why there had been so few translations. I'd read that passage what felt like ages ago. Was I finally beginning to understand?

Lights flashed from the river. I heard the clanking and grinding of cranes. The dredging had started up again.

"A bridge," Abby suddenly said, pointing.

On the northern edge of the battleground was a long stone bridge with seven arches built over a flowing tributary of the Red River.

"Long Bridge," said Chad. "There was a skirmish there at about dusk the first day of battle. The Long Bridge Skirmish. Hundreds of cavalry were killed."

"You probably don't want to remember what happened there," said Jem quietly, peering at me. "But I think you've got to, Captain."

And suddenly I *did* remember. The Long Bridge Skirmish wasn't a skirmish at all. It was a massacre. And Ulysses' men were the victims. Close to four hundred cavalry troops were ambushed there by Yankee guerrillas.

I snapped open the old cartridge box that held Ulysses' book and found the right lines.

Chains meant to bind, tore hooves asunder. We charged
Across the bridge. A few of us — no more — passed by
Before those chains pulled taut across the stone,
And sent both horse and man to ambush and to
*   death below.*

But that was poetry. I also remembered — really remembered — the mayhem on the stones. The shots. The sudden attack. Sabers hacking. Rain. Blood. Confusion.

I shook.

Abby put her hand on my arm. "Derek —"

Jem motioned upriver. "That's the most important thing I need to show you. Your manufactory. That phantom took you away."

Okay, my mind was reeling with enough stuff — - totally, completely unbelievable stuff — and now that word again: "phantom."

Following Jem's gaze, I saw a squat building of blackened brick hugging the shore a couple of miles up the river. It was barely visible in the driving rain.

"We're ready to fight," Jem said slowly, his voice sounding through the open hole in his cheek. I couldn't help shuddering. "Hundreds will follow you to close the Wound and stop the Grand Return."

Jem didn't have to tell me what the Grand Return was. Looking down on the sodden fields, I could imagine it just fine. A huge translation. *The* huge translation.

I didn't have time to get too carried away before a crazy reenactor rode a horse like a banshee through the woods below, calling the men to the first reenacted skirmish. The fake soldiers cheered.

"Oh, right. My other job," the guide muttered. He loped to the nearby rope and gave it a tug. The bell clanged overhead.

Dawn? Already? But it was still as gray as night.

"It was raining that day, too," I said under my breath. "And pitch-black."

Ronny turned to me. "How do you know that?"

"I . . . it's in the poem," I said.

I didn't know if it was in the poem or not. But how do you say "I remember that day in 1864. It was the day I died"?

Uh-huh. Right.

"It's time," said Jem. He spun on his worn heels and hurried down the wooden stairs. I followed.

◄| SIX |►

Train of Wagons

"Derek, I just got up here," Abby called after me as I started down the stairs.

"You can sure stay," I heard the guide say.

"Save it, Frodo," she said, and I almost smiled as I continued on my way, while Ronny hung back, scanning the ground below. "Derek, wait for me —"

But Jem had reached the bottom of the tower and retreated quickly into the trees. I couldn't wait. I hurried after him. Going down the stairs was easier than climbing up them, at least.

The young soldier took giant steps through the sludge of soggy ground, keeping on the edge of the woods until he paused near the old barn I'd seen from the tower.

As I trudged toward the barn, a wagon filled with reenactors rolled out of the woods onto the big field. Another one followed it, and more after that. I counted at least twenty wagons before I saw Jem slide into the dark barn through a side door. I glanced back. Abby and Ronny hustled through the rain and followed me inside.

The place smelled like rotten wood and vermin.

Jem headed to the dim back corner of the barn. Suddenly, the shadows shifted, and a half-dozen men stepped out next to Jem.

They were ghosts, too.

Every one of them was oddly familiar to me in some way — a pair of squinting eyes, a mustache, a cocked hat, grizzled cheeks, a limp, a pained grin. They all rippled vaguely through my brain.

The whole thing was insanity.

But when I saw those faces and remembered them, even just a little bit, I knew that something like a vault in my mind must have cracked. The train wreck had busted it open. Memories were oozing out. Lines of some old poem. Emotions. Knowledge. Facts. The ability to see and hear ghosts.

Terror.

Now that I was at the scene of Ulysses' greatest act, closing the Wound — and his death — everything was coming back to me in a flood.

"We have barns all over Shongaloo," said Ronny, glancing around in the dark. "But I hate this kind."

"What's wrong with it?" Abby asked, shivering.

"It's h-h-haunted," he said, turning away from the ghosts. Even though Ronny couldn't see them, he could tell where they were. He stared sullenly out the open barn door, watching the wagons pass. He was decaying on the outside — I could see the growing patch of gray flesh on his neck — but he was decaying inside, too. He couldn't see or hear the ghosts anymore. And now he stuttered.

I could see *and* hear the ghosts. Lucky me.

They tottered back and forth, every black eye on me.

"So the Grand Return is happening now? Today?" I asked. "Is that what's coming? More Legion soldiers? How can anyone stop it?"

"Wild horses galloped onto the Long Bridge," one ghost said. "Horses and men crashed off the side, into the water. You remember that. That's how I died."

"Some say K set up that ambush," a second put in.

"K?" I repeated. "Who's K?"

Ronny spun around. "What? Did you say K? Is K here?"

A tall, hatless ghost with one arm spoke next. "He's around. I saw him sneaking among the rocks at Cross Crag."

A new character? I wanted to hurl again. I clutched Ulysses' book and remembered a phrase from the poem.

. . . the nameless one . . .

I turned to Ronny. "They say K is here. Who is he?"

"He's . . . something different," Ronny said quietly.

"Evil?" asked Abby, quick to jump in. "Is K evil? Is he in the Legion?"

"I never found out," Ronny said, pacing through the barn door, in and out of the rain. "Maybe, maybe not. I met him once in the afterlife. I didn't like him. No one did. Maybe he wants to get rid of the First. Maybe he wants to get rid of others *for* the First. Who knows?" Ronny's eyes narrowed. "K learned to mask his sound in the afterlife, so we would n-n-ever even know if he was here. . . ."

"That boy's right," said Jem, his eyes shrinking. "K is trouble."

Ronny muttered under his breath and stepped fully into the rain. He hunched his shoulders, turning his head and trying to listen. He took a step away from the barn. Another step.

"Ronny, don't you dare leave us," said Abby.

"I r-r-remember him," Ronny stammered. "If he's on the battlefield, he could lead us to the First." He turned to face me. His drenched skin darkened by the moment. "I can't see ghosts anymore, I can't hear the First, but I can try to find K. Maybe he'll r-r-emember me. Maybe he'll show himself to me. I'm going out there."

"Ronny, no," said Abby, moving into the rain and grabbing his arm. "We shouldn't split up. Don't —"

But I knew Ronny would go.

"I g-g-gotta," he said. "It's the only thing I can think to do. Derek, read that b-book!" He stumbled down the wagon path, toward the outcropping called Cross Crag, and was gone.

Abby groaned softly, looking at me. I just stood there. Why didn't I rush after him?

I wanted him with me. I *needed* him with me. He was Ronny, my brother! Except that he wasn't, not really. He wasn't Ronny, and I wasn't Derek. Everything was falling apart, and he was just one of the pieces.

I didn't know what to do. I didn't know anything.

One of the ghosts broke into my thoughts. "You're the special one," he said. "You bleed. They say the First bled, too."

A short man with black hair added, "Only two of you bleeders so far."

That ran through my veins like ice. I was getting used to the feeling.

The ghost with the black hair rested his hand on the shoulder of a figure in a gray cap, who seemed to be kneeling on the hay. His head was only waist high.

"I fell with the First at Cerro Gordo," that ghost said. He shuffled forward awkwardly in the hay. I saw that he had only the top half of his legs.

I tried not to look.

"He was a colonel in the Mexican War in 1847," the legless ghost went on. "And a madman, and a savage. They call him the First because he was the first one who came back."

"Tell me about him," I said, moving closer to the ghosts. Abby followed, hearing only my side of the conversation.

"For fifteen years, the First rose in the ranks of the Legion in the afterlife," the soldier without legs told me. "Before him, the Legion was just a rabble of dead souls. But he pulled them together and led a big revolt against the good souls. Then the Wound tore open, and he escaped. Captain Ulysses discovered him. But when Ulysses closed the Wound, the First remained."

"He *remained*?" I said. "Here?"

I heard Abby gasp softly. "Who?"

"Fat Henry, tell the captain what happened to you," said Jem. He motioned to a tall, gaunt man — the opposite of fat — standing like a statue in the corner. The tall ghost stepped forward, pawing the side of his head again and again. It was like a nervous tic.

"I can never forget it," Fat Henry said in a soft voice. "He took my body for a while, used it up. He found another."

The man didn't focus on me. His eyes, dead black, looked like they were glistening with tears.

It didn't make sense. I shook my head. "How did he do it?"

"He took my body for a while, used it up. He found another. He took my body . . ."

"Derek, I hear a noise outside," said Abby, tugging on my sleeve. "Trucks, maybe. Do you hear them?"

I blinked, looked at her. "Yes . . . but . . ."

"It's them, isn't it?" she said. "The Legion. They're finally here."

I tried to understand. It wasn't working. Too much at once.

I turned back to Jem. "Are you saying the First came back during the Battle of Cemetery Bend, and he stayed? For over a hundred and forty years?"

"He took my body for a while . . . ," Fat Henry repeated.

"What's happening?" asked Abby.

"The ghosts are saying that the First stayed," I said. "He was trapped out of the Wound — on this side. He took over one body after another."

Her eyes narrowed, and her face clouded. "You mean he kept killing people? So he could inhabit a new body whenever he needed one? That's . . . horrible. But there would be proof, wouldn't there?"

"Seriously? Proof?" I shook my head. "There's an opening to the afterlife and dead guys are pouring through, and you want to be logical?"

"Don't snap at me! I'm your friend here. Your only friend, if you don't count your snooty brother, who couldn't wait to take off and look for S or W or whoever."

"K," I said.

"Whatever. My mother told me to stick with you. And maybe we'll never even see Ronny again."

The thought jarred me.

The ghosts drifted off. Jem stood just outside the barn doorway. Heavy rain poured through him.

"Now to where the phantom was born," he said.

"What?" I said. That word again.

"By the river, through the stones. It's in the book." With that, Jem walked into the rain.

What was that supposed to mean? Having a ghost guide was helpful, I guessed, but I couldn't help thinking that I would have liked Jem more if he wasn't so cryptic.

Clutching the cartridge box that hung from my shoulder, I turned to Abby. "Jem says I have to go —"

Without any further explanation, I walked straight out of the barn after the ghost. Abby followed. Rain drenched us all over again.

I didn't know what "through the stones" meant. I had no idea what I would find by the river, either. But I knew I had to go.

⊰ SEVEN ⊱

A Poem of the Long War

I couldn't see much in the pelting rain. It wasn't easy to follow a ghost in this mess.

We tramped along the edge of the woods to where it opened onto Bloody Meadow. I pressed the cartridge box tightly to my side, knowing that the book was safe inside. Abby scrambled along behind me.

Jem stumbled toward the river, muttering to himself about the book. It was all in the book.

I'd read only snatches of it so far. I hadn't exactly had quiet time for story hour. But I knew I would have to read the whole poem before the day was over if I was ever going to figure this out. For now, I'd just have to rely on what I could remember. The pouring rain wasn't the best place to pull out an old book, but I'll tell you what I know.

The Ghost Road: A Poem of the Long War was more than a thousand lines long. The fine black-ink handwriting that began the poem soon gave way to more of a quick scrawl. By the end, the writing was frantic — sometimes illegible.

The poem was divided into four parts, which he wrote over three years until his death. Across the first page were faint block letters, slightly slanted: *Amaranthia — 1861*. An inch or so down from that heading, Ulysses began his poem.

Within your crimson walls, I was an angel child;
From room to room I floated in your wingless window
    light . . .

He went on about his childhood, which was happy and sunlit. I'd already memorized those words.

                           O Amaranthia,
When on your blossoming fields I played young captain,
With my boyhood mate, young Thomas Bell —

Riding our ponies breakneck o'er the hills,
Or playing boats and underboats along the riverbank
(His dubbed the Crux, *mine* Spectre *was) —*

We were immortal sons of your Elysium,
But little knew what lay ahead for us — what
    lay ahead!

There was more, about his family, his days in school as he and Tom Bell grew up, college in the North, his sweetheart, and then the day that he and Tom rode off to war.

I'd read enough Civil War history to know that both sides, the Union and the Confederacy, predicted that victory would be theirs easily. Except that there was no victory. Not for either side. Fighting dragged on through four long years.

I wiped the water from my face.

I had to duck off the path when a troop of reenactors burst noisily out of the woods and onto the field. Abby darted after me. But Jem kept striding away. The reenactors couldn't see him. The troop hustled along the edge of the woods until they reached a stone wall. They followed it to a break, slipped behind it, and went on their way.

"Derek," said Abby, "this is weirding me out. Can you please say something? Don't pull a Ronny on me, okay? Where are we going? Are we lost?"

I turned to look after Jem and spotted something through the trees. A few plaques had been set up, by battlefield restoration groups, I guessed.

"We're not lost," I said.

Beyond the trees was a thin, flat stone, cracked and leaning. There were other stones all around, some upright, some flat on the ground. Rain scoured the words on their mottled faces.

Now I knew what "through the stones" meant.

"The cemetery."

⊰ EIGHT ⊱

Dead Boy Walking

Pushing through the overgrown shrubs and vines, I saw rows of marble markers snaking into the distance, one after another down to the water. Jem made his way slowly across the cemetery.

He was talking to the stones.

A low growl in my bad ear told me that Erskine Cane was getting closer. Waldo Fouks, too. And behind them both was that constant rumbling — lower than the deepest human voices — of the gathering Legion.

They were almost at the battlefield.

"There must be thousands of graves here," Abby said quietly, looking around.

It was true. Jem peered down at one stone, then collapsed to his knees, the rain still washing through him. From where I stood, I could read the name etched on the stone — Frederick Ross. Jem's brother?

"He died in a ditch," Jem said over his shoulder. "They all died in ditches."

Old Tom and I, unhorsed, retreated to the meadow,
Its deep-gouged earth, all ditches, channeled by the
  rain . . .

"Derek?" said Abby. She could tell that something was going on with me.

My skull ached from the flood of memories, the poem. I felt attacked. Ulysses was always there, talking in my head. I hated it. I hated him. If I didn't hate him, he would take over, wouldn't he?

And if he took over . . . who would I be?

Abby broke into my thoughts again. "Derek, will you please talk to me?"

So I talked.

Even though I tried to hold them back, the words spilled out. I told her how Union soldiers descended on Ulysses and his friend Tom during the battle. They flew out of the woods, across the sodden ditches of the meadow.

"Ulysses drew his cavalry saber," I said. "It belonged to his grandfather. A Union soldier knocked him back with his rifle. The saber broke when he fell. Three Federals jumped at him, but Tom Bell grabbed the broken saber and thrust himself between the soldiers and his friend."

Abby watched me closely. "This is in the poem?"

"Yes," I said. It was, but it was also burned into my memory somewhere. I knew that now. "And then, somehow, the saber — Ulysses' broken saber — flew up. Tom Bell screamed. The saber cut deep."

Abby turned pale. "Gross."

"It was," I said, seeing the scene in front of me. "Tom fell into a ditch and went still. Ulysses watched the ditch water bubble and splash over his face."

Abby shook her head slowly. I went on.

"After that, another bunch of Union soldiers charged out from the woods, and Ulysses ducked behind the wall over there to hide. I remem — Ulysses wrote about those cold minutes, waiting for the troops to move off. When they finally left, he searched the bodies lying in the field. He stumbled over the flooded ground until he heard a sudden splash and saw a man lurch up —"

Though it was getting weirder by the minute, I remembered the scene and the words at the same time.

Tom grasped my arm, ferocious as some maddened animal,
Bellowing, "I live! I live! I live!"

And that was it. What Ulysses saw in that moment was the first translation. My knees wobbled with the realization.

Was that really the way it had happened? Had Thomas Bell become the First? Was it his best friend?

He whirled my broken saber in the air and sheathed it
  on his side.

"A keepsake, if I may," he said, "of having died."

"You are welcome to it, my friend," I said to him.

My racing mind was interrupted by the sound of sobbing. Jem's face was in his hands as he quaked at his brother's grave. His tears mingled with the rain.

I knew how he felt.

I remembered feeling the same way at Ronny's empty tomb in New Orleans. Only . . . it *wasn't* my brother's tomb, was it? Ronny was Virgil Black by then, and I was already Ulysses Longtemps. We weren't brothers at all.

We were nothing, only I hadn't known it yet.

I turned to Abby. I had put it off for too long. I had to tell her. I had to get it out of me. It was like throwing up all over again.

"Abby . . . that happened to me, too."

She stepped back, pushing her hair out of her face. "What? You know someone who died like Tom, then came back? You mean Ronny?"

"No. Me." I could barely look at her.

"What?"

A light from the dredger flashed across the cemetery. Jem bolted to his feet. He stumbled away through the gravestones like a frightened deer and plunged into the woods toward the riverbank. "Come on," he called. "No time!"

Groaning voices sounded from the road behind us. "Hurry," I said to Abby. We'd have to finish our conversation later. It was just as well.

I hustled after Jem from one crooked path to another. We ran for what felt like half an hour before we wound up on the rutted streets at the outskirts of Cemetery Bend. The village was a nothing of a place. But once I stepped through the fog and onto those streets, it felt like I had walked the route a hundred times.

"Derek!" Abby's call came from far back. The girl was recovering from a fractured ankle, after all. "Where are we going?"

I slowed. "A building by the river. Jem says it's where the phantom was born."

I couldn't see her face clearly from this far away, but I was pretty sure she rolled her eyes. "Oh, great. What does that even mean?" she said.

I didn't answer, just waited for her to catch up and followed Jem down a crooked street. Most of it wasn't paved. Brick buildings lined the street on one side, and the river was on the other.

I thought I heard a splash, turned, and saw something moving beneath the water just beyond the street. What was it? A shape? A face?

Whatever it was, it was keeping pace with me.

A voice spoke: *We are ready!*

I tried to keep a grip on my sanity. Easier said than done. Abby didn't see the shape. Didn't hear it speak. Of course she didn't.

I had to tell her about me. Then she'd understand. "Abby, something happened to me —"

"Look," she interrupted, staring past me to the end of the street.

A solitary black building loomed — half piled up the riverbank, half falling into the water.

We were there.

⊰ NINE ⊱

The Manufactory

"What is it?" Abby asked. "Some kind of factory?"

Jem hovered in the shadows of the building.

"Manufactory," I said. It was a word I'd never said out loud before. "Well, yeah. It's a factory."

It was a low, thick, brick-faced structure built down a slope from the road. One story fronted the road, but there were two on the waterside.

Abby started walking toward the building. "What's inside?"

"I don't know," I said, falling into step with her.

But didn't I?

I tugged the Ulysses book out of the cartridge case. I flipped the pages, past the part where Ulysses left home to fight.

The second section was called *The Manufactory 1862–1863* and was scratched in several different-colored inks. The pages were greasy, creased with dirt. Just scanning them, I knew that the poem focused on Ulysses becoming a cavalry officer, and followed him through the first two years of fighting.

I tried to be all things — poet, thinker, husband, officer,

Surgeon, friend. But like my men, these died off one by one

Until everything I was . . . was just a soldier.

I wondered what Ronny might have been if he hadn't become "just a soldier," fighting the dead in the afterlife. Was that what I was supposed to be, too?

Further on, I read how something had happened to change Ulysses.

Then came a light into my darkness. A memory and vision

Of some one thing to end this war and drive it from our land.

Thus boy-I-was and man-I-am combined. And I began my work.

I've already told you that I didn't like poetry. It was, of course, kind of a sick joke that Ulysses had turned out to be a poet, because I'd always hated the stuff so much. But were lines like these the "code" my mother had told me I had to decipher?

What did the guy mean — *boy-I-was and man-I-am combined*?

Ugh.

"Derek?" said Abby. "I see a light inside."

I glanced up, but turned back to the pages.

"Listen to this." I read aloud as we walked.

"*I chose a secret building by the shore — my manufactory.*

And kept a vigil lonely and alone. Me and my phantom.'"

"Okay, but who's the phantom?" Abby asked.

I didn't know, and said so, though the word meant something to me. Reading that scrawled word on the yellowed page, I felt like I was dropping quickly through water.

"Are we going in or not?" Abby rubbed her arms. "It's cold out here."

There was a reason for that — besides the rain. Jem was standing behind Abby's shoulder, shaking his head. "She sticks with you, doesn't she?"

I pulled Abby away from him and approached the river side of the building. Jem walked past and vanished through the wall.

The bricks were uneven. The mortar had long ago cracked and spilled out between them. The roof tiles were slate, mostly chipped, a few missing. The place looked long-abandoned — except for that single dull glow against the high windows. It cast a dirty yellow sheen onto the pavement.

"How do we even get into this place?" Abby asked. "The door has no handle on it."

I tried *not* to remember, but I couldn't help myself. "Stand back. Please."

Reaching over our heads, I pressed my fingers against the doorframe and moved them slowly along the rough red mortar. I found what I was looking for and pulled. An iron lever shifted. The door popped open an inch or two.

Abby whistled. "Well, look at you, the expert in old buildings. . . ."

All at once, the door swung wide, and the barrel of a gun was pressed against my forehead.

"Hands up! Or I'll shoot you where you stand!"

⊰ TEN ⊱

By a Candle's Flame

I put my hands up. Abby slipped into the shadows.

Smart girl.

"That's right, son. Keep them high. I might be little, but from this range, my pistol won't miss!"

The woman beyond the door *was* little, but she kept the pistol pressed firmly against my head. She was about my mother's age and wore thick glasses and a slouchy beret.

"That will probably misfire," I said, surprising myself.

The woman blinked. "Excuse me? What was that?"

Yeah, what *was* that? I can't tell you how, but I recognized the gun. Unlike the replicas the reenactors used, this one was real. But the pistol happened to have a problem that I knew about. Somehow.

"That's a Colt Navy revolver," I said. "Damp air makes them jam."

The woman looked at the gun in her hand. "It does?"

I nodded. "That was the joke about them. It's a Navy revolver that doesn't work when it's wet."

"Now, that's just weird, Derek," Abby said, coming into the light of the open door. "How would you know that?"

When the woman saw Abby, she jerked the pistol at her but finally lowered and uncocked it. "Hmpf. I guess most thieves don't bring their girlfriends with them —"

"Girlfriends?" Abby snorted. "There are no girlfriends here!"

She said it as if it were a bad word. But there were bigger things than my ego to deal with now.

"You're a spicy thing, aren't you?" the woman said. "This place is off-limits to those beer-bellied reenactors. Don't want them pawing at my work. But you kids come along in, out of the rain. Though it's not so funny, me holding a gun on you. I've been attacked twice — once at home, once in my hotel. Fire at the hotel that time." She turned and disappeared inside, leaving the door open behind her.

A fire? Abby and I looked at each other. I knew we were thinking the same thing —Erskine Cane, the arsonist. Why would he go after *her*?

But when I saw the long room of the workshop inside, I got my answer. I knew it. I had spent many hours in that very room.

Nightly in that long room, my courage drained,
  Guttering like a failing candle flame . . .

My knees buckled under me.

"Whoa, you okay?" the woman asked.

"He's just a little wobbly," said Abby, holding me up.

"On account of?"

"On account of Derek sees ghosts," Abby said matter-of-factly.

"Ghosts?" The woman blinked again, then laughed heartily. "I see ghosts all the time!" She laid the revolver down on a workbench. "My name is Mercedes Bloom. Professor Bloom to my students. I teach Civil War history at Tulane in New Orleans. History is full of ghosts."

Yeah, not quite the same. Little did she know that a ghost was sitting at her desk that very moment. I glanced at Jem, then back at Professor Bloom.

"How did you find my secret place?" she asked.

"Yeah, Derek," said Abby, "how *did* you find this place?"

My eyes were drawn to the shadows at the far end of the room. My heart thudded, then skipped.

And yet I pressed myself with keenest eye and agile
  hand,
To craft a lung of iron, an iron crypt, whose breath was
  merest silence.

I knew then what stood in the shadows.

"The *Phantom* is a submarine," I said aloud.

"So! You've heard of my work!" Smiling cautiously, Professor Bloom pulled a lever on the wall. A large tubular object was instantly bathed in spotlight.

Abby drew in a breath. "Holy submarine, Batman."

Fifteen feet from nose to tail, the *Phantom* looked like a giant iron cigar. Fins jutted out along the sides. A cone on top was chopped flat like a hat.

The hull was made of plates rounded and fastened by big rivets and thick gobs of hasty welding. There was a porthole the size of a pie plate on the brow of the rounded nose. It looked like a glass eye. A propeller pointed downward at an angle from the rear.

"This is a replica of an old submarine called the *Phantom*," said Professor Bloom. "It was built in 1864 —"

"By Ulysses Longtemps," I cut in. I couldn't stop shaking.

Professor Bloom's eyebrows shot up. "How do you know that name?"

"I'm . . . a Longtemps," I said.

Little did she know.

Professor Bloom whistled quietly. "A Longtemps! Then you'll know that even though Ulysses was a captain in the Louisiana cavalry, he was also a wealthy engineer. Something happened, I don't know exactly what, but he designed and built the *Phantom* on his own time to help the war effort. Took him two years. It was only used once. And Longtemps died on its maiden voyage, drowned after it exploded underwater."

Part of me trembled to hear all that from a stranger.

My fingers tingled as I reached out to touch the iron. I traced the head of each rivet, cupped my hands around the porthole frame, and peeked inside. The replica was amazingly close to the submarine lodged in my memory — the one I hadn't even remembered at all until a minute before.

"Up until last year, we thought there was nothing left of the sub but these plans," said Professor Bloom, gesturing to blueprints spread out over her workbench. "Then I actually found part of the submarine about two miles downriver of here." She pointed to a chart of the Red River tacked to the wall.

I shook even more.

Two miles? Was that where the Wound was?

"I started researching the *Eastport* disaster, then discovered a rusted metal fin that matched the plans," she said. "It had fused somehow with the bedrock of the river, as if by incredible heat. Impossible to retrieve. Luckily I took its measurements. With all the dredging, it's impossible to know if it's still there."

"Uh-huh," I said, moving around the submarine, trying to listen to what she was saying. I hoped Abby was paying attention. My mind was falling backward in time. I imagined Ulysses hammering rivets, welding seams, setting the delicate instruments into the submarine's nose.

"The *Phantom* was revolutionary in several ways," the professor said, happy to have an audience. It reminded me of that moment on the train before the crash, when Dad described his love of trains.

A long time ago.

"The pneumatic bladders were invented in 1845," I said, blurting out some crazy words. Where had they come from? "Ulysses used them for buoyancy. The crew could either pump in air or pump out water."

Professor Bloom made a face. "You doing a report on your great-grandfather's old sub or something?"

"Or something," I said.

Spotting a computer on a small desk nearby, Abby gasped. "Oh my gosh, can I go online?" She barely waited for Professor Bloom's answer before sliding into a chair at the worktable and plugging her phone into an empty charger.

The professor shrugged. "Knock yourself out."

I knew what Abby was looking for — something to verify that the First had stayed behind after

Ulysses had closed the Wound. I already believed he had — but Abby needed more. Discovering a pattern of odd deaths around Cemetery Bend over the last century and a half might be the way to convince her — and others.

I couldn't take my hands off the submarine, as if I thought it would give me answers. But when I noticed a small plastic propeller on the back, beneath the larger, copper one, I stopped cold. "This isn't right."

"There's a small engine," Professor Bloom explained. "I want to pilot the sub underwater, but the university won't let me take it out unless there's a backup engine. All the old subs sank, you know. The engine doesn't compromise the integrity of the design, just adds a safety backup." She hooted a laugh. "Never mind that there's only about a half hour of usable air in one of these things, anyway!"

"Is it sea-proof?" asked Abby, listening from the computer terminal.

"Seaworthy," I said.

"It doesn't need to be," I heard Jem whisper. "Not all that long, anyway." He was slumped on the floor now, with his eyes closed.

Professor Bloom smiled. "I've lowered her into the water, and she doesn't leak. After the dredger moves downriver, I'll take her out."

Abby clicked away on the computer, murmuring. "Oh man, oh man."

The clock on the wall chimed two. The high windows showed that the sky was even darker than before. Time was passing, but it felt like we were standing still.

Not the Legion, though. Their voices had been circling louder and louder since we'd heard the trucks when we were in the barn. What were they waiting for? How long before they would move across the fields, the woods, the swamps, the riverbank?

And what about Ronny? Was he finding anything out about this K person? How long had it been since he'd run off? Was he safe?

Too many questions.

"Do you want to sit inside?" Professor Bloom asked, popping open the *Phantom*'s top latch. "You can, if you like."

Abby looked over at the submarine. Jem did, too.

"I . . . thanks," I said. My hands shook as I climbed a short ladder and lowered myself into the top hatch. I slid inside the sub without difficulty. Was I getting thinner? Maybe all that running was paying off after all.

My breath quickened the second I sat on the cold iron seat. My throat constricted. I felt something brush my shoulder, then a movement next to me. I looked around the unlit submarine. Nothing.

Then another touch. Cold fingers on my arm. I turned again, quaking from head to toe.

A pale young face stared at me in the dark. The face had the faint shadow of a beard. Its owner was a few years older than Ronny, about the same age as Ulysses in the photo I'd seen. He had long brown hair, but his features weren't young and vibrant. He looked ghostly and gray with pain, aged before his time.

I'd known him forever.

"Tom . . . ?"

Abby called out from the computer. "Derek? You okay in there?"

"Tom," I whispered. He nodded once to me.

It was Thomas Bell, Ulysses' best friend. Old Tom. Every bit of their childhood together came rushing back to me. Playing by the riverbank, riding horses at Amaranthia. Then Tom's death in the ditch on Bloody Meadow, and the moment when he stood up and said, "I live!"

Now I wasn't just remembering what I'd read in the poem. These were my memories. Ulysses' memories.

I was momentarily afraid when Tom's face

appeared, but I knew immediately that the First wasn't inside him anymore.

"Tom," I whispered, "what happened in the submarine? The poem's unfinished. What really happened at the end —"

Old Tom seemed to breathe hard, without using any breath at all. Then he pawed the side of his head as Fat Henry had. I remembered then that they both had been killed the same way: in a flooded ditch with Ulysses' broken saber buried in the sides of their heads.

I heard a far-off noise outside the sub, outside the building. Someone was calling out. I couldn't hear what the voice was saying.

Tom stumbled over words, barely audible, and I had to move even closer. The air around him was frigid. I had never been so close to a ghost before. And now here we were, cramped inside this metal coffin, face-to-face.

"Blood . . . ," I thought he said.

"What?"

The faraway voice echoed in my ear again.

As I watched Tom, I felt like retching, or weeping, or drowning, or something. I kept remembering the broken saber, the wound on his head, the ditch.

He spoke up finally. "My . . . blood . . ."

All at once, Old Tom's face turned as pale as snow.

He clamped a hand over his sliced ear, then faded into nothing — but not before reaching out and touching my hand.

I gasped for air. I found none. I was drowning all over again, in no water this time. I reached for the hatch but fumbled it, and it slammed down over me, plunging me into darkness. I banged on the hull, screaming. I couldn't breathe.

Suddenly, the hatch popped up and Abby was there, dragging me out by my wrists. I collapsed to the floor. Professor Bloom had the phone to her ear. "Emergency —"

"No! Hang up, please!" Abby cried. "He has fits. It's okay. I know what to do. Hang up, please. Maybe some water?"

The professor hung up the phone and hustled off to another room to get a glass of water.

Abby leaned over me. "Are you going to make it?" Jem hovered in the shadows, watching.

"I'm okay. . . ." But I wasn't.

I realized now that the voice in my ear, so faint and far away, was Ronny's. He was calling out, crying, in trouble. And I heard him.

"Then listen," Abby whispered. "I think I found it. In 1927, 1960, and 1982. There were more, I bet, but I could only find those three. When the police discovered a body, someone went missing. When that person turned up dead, another person vanished. Derek, the First *did* survive —"

Glass exploded across the room. A smoking bottle flew through the broken window onto the floor and shattered. Jem vanished instantly.

Professor Bloom screamed. "Now we call 911!"

The door thudded and began to splinter. Abby grabbed her phone from the charger and dialed while the professor heaved her desk against the door.

"Leave me alone!" Professor Bloom cried out. "What do you people want?"

The room was so thickly lined with iron that it muffled the voices from outside. Was Cane out there? I couldn't tell, but I couldn't hang around to find out.

I heard Ronny's voice in my ear again.

"We need to get out of here!" I said, turning to the professor.

"I have to protect the sub!" said Professor Bloom. She tapped a code into a keypad on the wall. The submarine lowered into a tank beneath the factory, directly into the river. A thick iron plate sealed the top of the tank.

"You can only get to it from underneath," the professor said. "It'll be safe." She stuffed her own cell into her pocketbook, slung the bag over her shoulder, and ran for a circular staircase. "Up to the parking lot. My car —"

More glass shattered.

We bolted up the curving stairs and out a side door into an alley at the street level. Abby moved as quickly as she could on her still-healing ankle. We ran breathlessly, toppling over garbage cans. I heard a jangle of keys, and Professor Bloom grabbed us by the arms. "Both of you — inside!"

We all dived into her Jeep and roared away, not seeing who had attacked the factory. But Abby and I knew. The Legion was everywhere. Sirens already worked their way through the streets.

"To the battlefield," I said, trying to catch my breath. "My brother . . . needs help."

"I'm not even going to ask how you know that," Professor Bloom said, jerking the steering wheel. "Just fasten your seat belts!"

◄| ELEVEN |►

The Cemetery at the Bend

The battlefield wasn't that far away, but Professor Bloom had to follow the winding streets. Well, some of them. She raced the Jeep within an inch of its life, slicing corners, bounding onto sidewalks, skidding across lanes — just like Ronny would have.

"The more I think about this," the professor said, gunning through a red light, "the more I think you kids ought to be in school."

"It's summer," said Abby.

"Summer school, then," the professor said. "I'm getting out of here and going back to New Orleans. No way is grading papers as dangerous as this!"

She didn't know the half of it. I hoped she wouldn't have to.

The Legion's voices ground constantly in my ear now, sometimes loud, sometimes soft. But they never disappeared. The Legion was spreading across the battlefield, and I still didn't know exactly what they planned to do, or where to find the First.

Or what to do when I found him.

Ronny's voice was louder and closer . . . and he was in pain.

"Stop before you get to the police cordon," I said as Professor Bloom tore through the puddles flooding Swamp Road.

The Jeep splashed into a rut and splashed back out again. "End of the line," said the professor, sliding to a muddy stop a few hundred yards from the battlefield. "You want me to stay?"

"No," I said, scrambling out of the Jeep and closing the door behind me. "You should get as far away as possible."

The moment the professor roared off, Abby and I ran through the woods and past the tower, not stopping until we reached the cemetery fence. We heard groaning and branches cracking.

"Ronny?" I called.

There was a flash of light from among the tombstones, then the sound of hooves fading into the distance. By the time we got to Ronny, he was alone. He sank into the rain-softened ground on one knee. His left arm dangled, limp, by his side. A smell hung in the air, but it wasn't Ronny's smell of decay. It was different. A chemical odor, it smelled odd, thick, sharp, and disgusting — even in the rain.

"Who was it?" I asked, kneeling next to him.

He turned his face to me. One pupil was large and wild, the other as tiny as the head of a pin. His shirt was cut to ribbons at his shoulder. I saw slice marks on his skin, but not a trace of blood. There never was with Ronny.

Abby and I helped him to his feet. He leaned against a tree trunk.

"K is on the field somewhere. The s-s-spy. I w-was following him," he said. "He lured me here. I think it was a trap. You never know with K. But K wasn't here when I arrived. The other was here instead."

"Can you move your arm?" asked Abby, scanning him for other injuries.

"The other was here instead," he repeated. "He came at me from behind. I think there were ghosts here. I didn't see them." He turned to me. "Your g-g-ghosts, Derek."

My ghosts? Had he guessed that I was Ulysses? Did he know what my mother had told me? Or was he just thinking of Jem and the others?

Ronny shot a glance to the left, and I followed it with my eyes. Three or four ghosts lingered in the darkness under the pines. They were the ghosts from the barn. Ronny's eyes darted back and forth, but he still didn't see them.

"I th-think the ghosts spoke, but they couldn't do

anything," he went on. "The darkness was too heavy for them."

"The darkness?" Abby repeated. "Ronny, who fought you?"

But I already knew.

Feeling a weight of darkness wash over me,
I took Tom's shoulders in my hands . . .

Ronny's cheek darkened as he spoke. "I could b-barely touch him. My fingers screamed to f-f-fight him off. Derek, it was him. The F-f-first. Evil."

I shuddered. "You saw his face?" In my mind I saw a mass of gray, mottled skin. But it merged with the face of Tom Bell. I tried to focus. "Ronny, you saw him?"

He shook his head, grimacing. "I c-couldn't l-l-look."

Ronny's neck was almost completely black now. He caught me glancing at it.

"Am I t-talking right?" he said suddenly.

"No," said Abby. "You need to rest —"

"The Legion came for us at the factory," I said, changing the subject. "Ulysses built a submarine. The *Phantom*. There's a replica —"

"So what?" Ronny snapped, pushing both of us away and standing on his own. "A toy boat? There are k-killers on the field!"

"I think it means something about the Wound," I said.

We heard engines roaring and shots — real shots — and grunting and the splashing of men falling in water. The first sounds of attack. The Legion had started to push reenactors toward the river.

"The battle has s-s-started," said Ronny.

Troops of soldiers were moving into position, exactly as they had in 1864. The massacre in the flooded field, the ambush on the bridge — all the forces were riding and running to where they needed to be.

The pinging of real musket fire in the trees came then, followed by wild yelling. A brigade of reenactors ran out of the woods into the cemetery.

"Get out of here!" I yelled at them.

"Who are you guys?" one middle-aged man with glasses cried, throwing a look of terror over his shoulder. They all ran faster.

I dragged Ronny to the ground and pulled Abby with us.

Smoke swirled as thick as clay around the men, washing out from the trees behind them like waves of fog.

"Retreat?" yelled one. "But the directions say we advance two miles —"

Were some of the fake soldiers still playing?

Didn't they know?

"Get out of here!" I yelled, standing. "The attackers are real!"

And there they were.

The translated dead stumbled out from the trees. I recognized tourists from the bayou, townspeople from New Compson. Their dark shapes moved relentlessly, ragged but determined and swift. Some had rifles. Others had swords, and they used them.

I saw Santa, the bearded man from the campfire. His face was no more than a tangled gray beard, his mouth screaming a big dark O of panic. His yell joined with other noises in the confusion — running footfalls, crying, laughing, bursts of musket fire, momentary silence, and a storm of howls. A mass of fake soldiers ran like madmen right at us.

They rushed among the gravestones, leaping over and around them. I had to step aside, was pushed down, tried to get up, was pushed away. "No —"

Ronny cried, "Derek, get back here! Abby!"

I reached for Abby's arm. But she was torn away from me in the rush of bodies.

"Abby!" I cried. "Abby!" I called over and over, stumbling toward where I'd last seen her. Waves of men rushed past me, knocked me down again. I struggled to get up. There was a crash in the trees to my left. My bad ear rang uncontrollably. I could barely hear anything but the ringing.

I bolted in the direction the men had gone.

"Ronny!" I called out. "Abby —"

A horse galloped through the trees. Five horses. Ten. A cavalry troop overran the cemetery. I dashed aside and was suddenly alone in the dark.

"Abby! Ronny!"

I couldn't hear them. Above the ringing in my ear I heard the sound of musket fire in the distance and the thundering of hooves approaching again.

I ran.

⊰| TWELVE |⊱

Dead Quiet

Dark shapes moved in the woods on both sides of the cemetery. Men — living men — rushed among the gravestones and into the flooded ditches beyond. Some yelled, most ran, some even laughed, having no idea that their attackers were real or that their comrades were actually dying.

Water splashed over and over. The whole battlefield was soaked. Water was everywhere.

The translations had begun.

A troop of horsemen appeared on the far edge of the woods. These weren't weekend soldiers playing pretend. They wore the ashen faces of the dead.

"No, no, no . . ."

I spotted a rambling building on the edge of the cemetery. The stable I'd seen from the tower? Maybe Abby and Ronny had seen it, too. Holding the cartridge box tight under my arm, I ran, slogged low beside a stone wall, then lurched through the open field to the stable. I kicked open the door as if it were paper, and dived in before the dead saw me.

My brain was a mess. I needed time.

The stable had been converted into some kind of battlefield museum. Instead of housing horses, it was a house of war. And it was dead quiet.

No Ronny. No Abby.

Closed because of the reenactment, the rooms were nearly as dark as caves, with only grimy windows shedding a sick gray light. When my eyes adjusted to the dark, I made out display cases of documents, uniforms, weapons. I tugged at them. All locked. Bayonets and sabers stood in cases along the wall. Single-shot derringers and revolvers like Professor Bloom's were in a long set of cases, which ran the length of one side of the stable.

Outside, the cemetery was alive with shouts, grunts, thundering footsteps.

No, "alive" wasn't the right word. Not everyone making those noises was alive.

I peered around the stable, trying to distract myself, to gather my thoughts. On a pedestal beneath a gray window stood a tin model of the *Eastport.* What had Ronny called the *Phantom*? A toy? But it was more than that. If the explosion of the *Eastport* had caused the first Wound, had the *Phantom* somehow closed it?

I popped open Ulysses' cartridge box, pulled out the book, and pawed through the brittle pages. I flipped past the incident in the ditch. Past the First's translation into Tom. I wanted to read about the submarine.

> *Tom warns me of a thing he knows. That scuttled wreck,*
> *The* Eastport, *harbors secrets that will turn the war against us.*
> *His talk is veiled, he speaks in riddles, yet convinces me*
> *Of a mission two or three might undertake in secrecy:*
> *To blast that sunken ship to kingdom come.*

Tom had already been taken over by the First, and he wanted to go to the site of the explosion. Why? To make the hole bigger? To bring more of the Legion here? When did Ulysses realize this? When did he truly understand about the Wound?

> *Thus Tom and I, and he, the nameless one, enter the deep.*
> *The* Phantom *takes me into it, that lung of iron,*
> *Its nose and tail with many charges filled.*

"The nameless one?" I said aloud. Weirdly, I was comforted by the sound of my own voice. At least Ulysses hadn't taken over that. "K? Was K on the *Phantom* with Ulysses and Tom Bell?"

I turned to the end of the poem and found these lines on a page by themselves:

Confusion reigns as we approach the gaping Wound;
I steer and steer and steer and

Then nothing. *The Ghost Road* ended like that, in mid-line. How in the world was I supposed to —

A barrage of musket fire rattled in my good ear. Some shots sounded like hollow popping. Others were deeper, sharper — real shots.

I felt like crying. An insane, impossible war between the living and the dead was raging out there — and I was supposed to stop it!

With an unfinished poem?

With some ridiculous code?

Horses thundered past the stable. Horrified cries. The clang of steel.

I glanced at a saber in one display case. It wasn't for me. I picked up a chair and brought it down hard on the next case over. Glass flew everywhere. I grabbed a short folding dagger with a thick, almost tool-like blade. Don't ask me why. It seemed useful. I slipped it into my pocket just as a troop of mounted soldiers galloped by the busted stable door. I couldn't tell if they were living or dead, but I wasn't taking any chances. I ducked under the case, dragged it across the room after me, and used it to brace the door shut.

Chaos raged around the stable. I was being pulled back to the battle, and I was losing Derek Stone.

"But I *am* Derek," I said to the gray air. My voice was weak, pathetic. It sounded like I didn't even believe my own words.

I tried to remember what it was like to be me. The boy who'd started this story. The boy who lived in New Orleans.

"Derek, Derek, Derek," I whispered.

Breathing deeply, trying to calm down, I traced my finger across a framed map hanging on the wall nearby. I moved it from Alexandria to Bordelon — the train route — then from New Orleans to Bayou Malpierre to Baton Rouge to Coushatta to Cemetery Bend.

Would I ever be home in New Orleans again? It had been only a few days since I'd been there. But when you leave home, it always feels like forever since you've been there. You know what I mean.

My house on Royal Street was nothing but a burned-out shell now — Erskine Cane had seen to that. Uncle Carl was probably in a hotel somewhere, trying desperately to find me and Ronny. Big Bob Lemon, who'd helped me understand this insanity in the first place, was probably dead, though I didn't know for sure. And my father — what about him? I didn't even know.

No, there was nothing in New Orleans for me. I

doubted I'd ever see it again. It wasn't home anymore. Home was where Ronny and Abby were. But maybe even that would end today.

By end of day, I knew that dead love might be me.

An outburst of angry cries snapped me out of it again. I peeked through one of the windows. A troop of pretend Federals rushed past the cemetery's far wall toward the meadow. I'd wait for them to leave, then try to find Abby and Ronny. But what would we do? Where would we go? The First was out there. Time was running out.

None of the pieces were fitting together.

I noticed then that the wall map seemed to waver. The edges were tinged with red light. Was I losing my mind? That question almost made me laugh. But then there was an outline of a human shape on the map. The shape wobbled and grew larger as I stumbled backward.

"What —"

I felt the heat. The door behind me was on fire. Red flames licked up both sides of the doorframe and across the top, where they spread to the ceiling.

What I'd seen on the frame was a reflection.

Erskine Cane had found me.

The closest window burst into the room, spraying chunks of old glass and shards of wood across the floor. I shielded my eyes, but some glass caught me on the cheek and chin. I ran my hand across my face. I was bleeding.

"Throw me the book," Cane said, his face staring at me through the busted window.

A second wall was on fire, crackling with flame.

"Throw me the book!"

◄| THIRTEEN |►

Cross Crag

Smoke thickened in the room. I ran to the far end, found a sliding door, and kicked the latch, snapping it. Pushing the door aside, I entered the unconverted stables. There were three stalls — not big, but not on fire. They had that going for them, anyway.

"Throw me the book!"

I could hear Cane, but I didn't know where he was. I held the cartridge box even tighter.

The whine of voices sounded all around the building. It was a tinderbox. Air burned in my lungs. Smoke filled my nostrils. I started to cough and thought I'd never stop. Above the roar of flames I heard horses whinnying outside.

And then . . . a shape moved inside the stable.

"Get away from me!" I shouted. The shape stopped. Cane's voice was still farther away, echoing distantly in my ears. This wasn't him.

Was it K? Ronny had said he could disguise his sound so no one could find him.

I moved away from the shape. "Get away —"

"Keep down!" a voice shouted over the roar of flames.

The wall next to me exploded with gunshot. I dived to the floor. It smelled like earth and rats and hay. More shots.

The shape reached me, shook me, its voice whispering gruffly in my ear. "Derek!"

I tried to focus. "Ronny?" I said. No, that wasn't right. No smell.

Suddenly, I was lifted powerfully to my feet. My knees buckled, and I fell back down.

"Derek, it's me."

Wiping the blood from my forehead, I made out the face. Deep eyes. Grizzled chin. I looked down to see a thickly bandaged hand. It couldn't be.

"Dad?"

"Derek, get up! You're out of time!"

I struggled to my feet. Even in the light of the flames, my father looked like death.

"There's an outcropping of rocks outside," he said.

Cross Crag. I knew it. "Okay . . ."

"I saw the girl run to them."

"Abby?" I asked. "Is she —"

"We have to get to the rocks," Dad said. He took my arm in his good hand and tugged it to keep me crouched down. "Be smart now. Stay low."

He pulled me to the only wall that wasn't burning . . . and kept going. Boards splintered when his shoulder struck it. Planks fell. What was that? How had he become so strong?

"There!" Cane's voice roared. Waldo was close, too. And the one-armed conductor from the train crash was running toward us. I saw them, heard them all.

My dad and I fell to the mud and struggled up, slipping and sliding, stumbling toward the river. We kept the burning museum between us and Cane. The field was broken by a group of huge glacial boulders, clustered, with winding paths between. This was Cross Crag. Rain hammered the rocks as we dashed among them.

"Abby!" I called.

"Shhhh!" Dad snapped.

"You said she was here —"

"Quiet," he said, searching ahead, looking for the way between the stones. "Stay here." He darted off, crouching. A moment later, he was back and motioned to me. My knuckles scraped against the rocks as I ran to catch up. He pulled me farther among the boulders and then collapsed against one, its blackness glistening in the rain.

I wiped my face on my sleeve. "Dad, how did you

even get here? Mom said you followed me to Baton Rouge. She set off a bomb to scare you away —"

"Derek, your mother's gone," he cut in coldly. "Never mind her."

"Gone? Gone where? Dad —"

"Listen!" he snapped. The battle quieted for a moment. He looked at me carefully. "You know about me," he said. "Don't you?"

Without thinking, I slid down next to him and touched his bandaged arm. He didn't resist. I unwrapped the stained swaths of cloth. The stump was black, dry.

No blood.

My heart sank. My father was someone else.

"You died on land," I said. "You're decaying."

"At Bordelon Gap. I saw a man fall. I needed to return." He wrapped his arm again.

"You saw my *father* fall," I said.

"I had to come back. I was needed here."

"But when this all started, you told me to find Abby," I said. "You told me about the First. You helped me escape from Cane in New Orleans. You tried to save the tourists in Bayou Malpierre. You fought the dead guys. You're on my side —"

"I'm on *my* side," he said quietly.

That was it.

"You're K!" I should have known. It all made sense. And I felt a surge of hope.

"You're not just on your own side. In the sub, you helped Ulysses. You saved him from the First. Did you come to help Ulysses now?" I was still talking about Ulysses as if he was someone else.

He nodded slightly. "Like the older boy helped you."

"Right, the way Ronny came to help me," I said. "My brother, Ronny. You remember him. Your son?"

Only Ronny wasn't his son. Or my brother. This man wasn't my father, either. I kept thinking this way, but it was all wrong. What I had thought was a family for years was now only a group of strangers. Dead strangers.

"You were in the bayou," I prompted. "You were there that night. With Mom."

He pushed the wet hair out of his eyes. "I don't remember that so clearly now. That was your father. I remember some things. He followed her and fired shots to keep the dogs away. He never knew what really happened there until after the train accident and I was inside him."

I heard howling from the fields. It wasn't human. We didn't have much time.

"How much does the Legion know?" I asked.

"The First told Cane that you were Ulysses. Everyone needed you to understand the book. But now it's too late. I need it."

"*You* need it?" I said, my voice rising. "What for? Did you save me from that burning building just now so you could get the poem?" I swung the cartridge box behind my back. "You tried to gain my trust just to get the book?"

Did K want the book for what it said, or for some other reason? Was there something else in it that I'd missed?

"They'll take it," he snapped. "You may not get away. I will. I don't want to hurt you, but you need to give me the book. There's no time to explain."

I climbed to my feet. The stable was an inferno now. The howling moved closer, but I couldn't see Cane or any of the others. I had a chance to run for it. Maybe. "No."

"No?" he spat. It was hard to see my dad like this — angry at me. "You care about Abby, don't you?"

Low blow. "Where is she?" I asked.

"The First has her," he said.

"I don't believe you."

"I led you to the book!" my father burst out. "Step

by step. I told you to find the girl, because I knew her mother had been telling her things. She'd know where the book was. And she did!"

A clatter rang out behind us. I spun and tried to run between the boulders, but couldn't find the way out. There was a sudden explosion over our heads. Rocks slammed my shoulder. My bones screamed. More rocks thudded behind me, and more, and more. One struck my knee hard, jamming it against the ground. I saw Cane's face. He was crawling over the boulders toward me.

"Come here!" Dad reached for my arm but caught the strap of the cartridge box instead and tried to pull me to him. When the strap broke, I realized he wasn't pulling me to him at all.

"No!"

He tore the cartridge box from my hands and slid away. "I need it! You'll never get out —"

He was gone, out of the rocks and through the trees, vanishing like a ghost. I was alone.

The howling came closer.

A second explosion boomed. I shielded myself and threw a loose rock in Cane's direction. He ducked, and I dragged myself away as fast as I could.

I got beyond the boulders somehow, stumbling into the open meadow. My knee throbbed. Was it broken? No, just twisted. I could still move it. Hot pain. A sense of something grinding in the joint, liquid, bleeding under the skin.

I heard the howling again. Only it was so close I knew what it was this time. Dogs.

I turned. White forms galloped across the meadow — right at me.

Waldo's bayou dogs.

I heard his voice pierce the pouring rain now, urging them on. They chased me across the field. I fell into a ditch, dragged myself out, tumbled over the stone wall, and hobbled into the woods.

⊰ FOURTEEN ⊱

Tower Dogs

Ghost dogs. My chubby legs took over. I ran as fast as I could. The dogs gained on me, galloping through the trees. I heard their ravenous cries all the way to the observation tower, with Waldo shrieking and stumbling after them.

I staggered up the wooden stairs, trying to keep myself moving. My kneecap burned. My brain fired and misfired, a mass of sparks and explosions. I couldn't breathe. I couldn't think. I ran on sheer terror.

"I don't have the book!" I cried, but I barely made a sound over the yelping dogs and the pounding rain and the storm of battle.

I reached the top of the stairs and staggered onto the platform. The guide was gone. Good thing. The ghost dogs, loping white shapes, rushed right after me. When I turned and saw them face-to-face, I stood my ground. There was nowhere else to go.

"Come on!" I found myself screaming at them. "Come on!"

Ghosts can't hurt you; I knew that. Not in such small numbers.

They leaped across the platform at me. I didn't move. It took everything I had to stand there. I wanted to duck, hide. But they just blew across me like a frozen wind before vanishing in the rainy air.

Waldo scrambled up the stairs, feeling his way. He charged onto the platform. His stunted body was a wreck. Waldo had aged since he had been translated years before, but he hadn't grown much. Even though his shriveled body looked like a six-year-old's, inside it was the dead soul of a smuggler born two hundred years ago. He reeked of evil.

"I got you, Derek Stone!" he hollered.

I knew what he was after. "I don't have the book."

One-Arm, the train conductor from Bordelon Gap, clambered up the stairs behind Waldo. His face was gray with death. I backed against the railing, hunkered into a crouch.

"I don't have the book," I repeated.

They weren't into conversation.

Waldo lunged, a mad puppet, while the conductor faked to the side and kicked my battered knee. I stifled a cry and fell backward into the log railing. I heard the crack of wood. A sliver cut into my palm. Gunshots rang out on the ground. While my head was turned, I saw torches crossing the field, a dark mass of men heading to Long Bridge, beyond the woods.

I shifted to my right, faked the conductor, crouched left, and kicked his leg out. He went down hard. I knew he wouldn't stay down, but it was something. Then I knocked Waldo in the face with my fist and dodged past him. Spinning around, I took hold of his shoulders from behind.

"What is the First planning?" I yelled. "What will he do?"

"You can't stop the Grand Return," Waldo said smugly. "The First is more powerful than you can imagine. The dead will come. Tonight!"

"I'll stop him!" I cried.

"You bleed!" Waldo squeaked. "He bled —"

"So what? *Tell me* —"

"It's in the book!" he said.

I paused for a second. Bad idea.

One-Arm had found his footing and rushed at me with the guide's log-footed stool. I dodged and kicked Waldo in the shoulder. He wasn't ready, and tumbled backward down the stairs.

He screamed.

I swung around, grabbed hold of the stool, and jabbed it straight back at One-Arm's face. It struck his nose hard, and he let go. With his only good hand, he punched me in the gut, then grabbed my neck with his iron fingers. I felt light-headed.

Was he trying to cut me? To twist my neck until a coil of smoky fog escaped and I was gone? That was how the translated dead left this world for good. I didn't want to be one of them. I struggled to free myself.

All at once, there was a stinking gray cloud rising over us. Smoke. The tower was burning.

With one hand clawing at his, I bashed my other hand into the stump of the conductor's arm. He gargled in his throat and staggered back, freeing me for a minute. I looked over the railing. Cane was setting the wooden legs of the tower on fire with a pair of blazing torches.

"Cane! No!" One-Arm screamed. "I'm up here!"

The arsonist's face was as blank as Waldo's. The bayou boy was curled on the ground, but he looked up and laughed as if his blind eyes saw the fire and liked it.

One-Arm swung once more at me, pounding my bad ear, before he turned and jumped down the stairs, taking them three or four at a time. Cane didn't wait. He thrust both torches onto the stairs, then stepped away from the tower to watch the flames rise.

I was going to die. I was going to end right there. Except that I couldn't.

A word came to me, and time slowed. A single word. I wasn't sure if I'd thought of it or if *he'd* thought of it. Ulysses. But there it was.

Rope.

Had it come from the mind of the soldier seasoned by battle in the afterlife? Had it come from the leader of the resistance?

Rope.

Or had it come from Derek Stone? Chubby Derek from New Orleans?

Or . . . had it come from some new place? Ulysses as Derek? Derek as Ulysses?

Was this what I was becoming? Both of us?

Time returned to its normal speed. As the flames rose through the tower, barely slowed by the pouring rain, I turned.

The bell rope. Even as I grabbed it with both hands and pulled it quickly up through the tower, I knew the next step. I'd toss it over the side opposite Cane and Waldo. It wasn't long enough to reach the ground, but it was close. I'd have to jump and run.

Jump and run? Was I insane? That was Ulysses talking. I wasn't that brave. I'd fall to my death or have rope burns so bad I'd want to be dead.

But I didn't have a choice.

I dragged the heavy rope to the railing and flung it over the side. Both knees burned now. I heard them grinding as I wound my hands and arms around the rope and began to climb down.

What a heavy mess I was! Still, not as heavy as a week ago.

Fire leaped up the tower. The heat was incredible, but I spotted a path south through the woods and up the river to the manufactory. Thinking ahead already, as if I really would escape.

Ulysses had used the *Phantom* to close the Wound; I was sure of it. The book told how, and the book was gone, but the poem was in my brain. It had to be. I'd written it!

Cane circled the tower, looking past me, trying to see me at the top through all the smoke. *Moron.*

No, good moron. Keep looking up!

I reached the end of the rope and was still dangling about fifteen feet above the ground. My hands stung. The fire, still not on the back side of the tower, leaped straight up. The smoke and flames obscured me. I dangled like an idiot, trying to shorten the distance between me and the ground. Was I really going to jump?

The decision was made for me when the rope burned through at the railing, and I fell. I slammed to the ground. It was not soft. My left knee turned in. I screamed.

Cane was there in a flash, his eyes glinting. I wailed like an animal, and he yanked me up from the ground, one arm around my neck, the other jabbing my back again and again. I couldn't breathe. It couldn't happen this way! I had too much to do! Not like this!

Then a sharp blow, and my spine rang like a chime. I fell like a lead weight.

I had been captured.

Taken, as Cane had promised so long ago.

⊰ FIFTEEN ⊱

Shroud

My eyes wouldn't open. My mouth tasted like dirty coins. Blood. And wafting past me from somewhere, the faint odor of chemicals I'd smelled earlier in the cemetery.

Chemicals meant the First. And the First had Abby.

My hands were bound behind me. Moving my jaw, I realized that my mouth was sealed. My eyes were covered, my ears under a thick bandage.

I tried to yell. That hurt plenty, and it didn't do any good. The sound came rushing back at me, muffled.

"Shhh," was the reply.

Had I imagined it?

There was no other noise except a low grinding far below me and the *thump-thump-thump* of something closer.

I struggled in and out of consciousness. The poem drifted into and across my mind, like tidewater at the shore. The unfinished story.

Confusion reigns as we approach the gaping Wound;
I steer and steer and steer and

A thicker chemical smell came over me, making me nauseous. Crackling light appeared beyond my bandages. I felt something cold in the air and heard hissing voices. I tried to yell again. No answer. My legs were bent, unmoving. I realized that I was sitting in a chair. How many hours had passed? My weight heaved side to side. The floor was moving.

Was I on a ship?

I wedged open my lips and sucked in. My mouth filled with rags. I bit them — disgusting — and pulled them farther into my mouth with my teeth, gnawing the fabric. I expected someone to notice at any second. No one did. I ground the rags with my teeth again and again until I heard the tear of gauze. The bandage loosened, unwound from my mouth, eyes, and ears like a shroud, and peeled away.

Seconds went by. Nothing.

Gingerly, I opened one eye. Everything was a blur and my head ached, even though the light was dirty and dim. It felt like my eyes had been pressed back into my skull. Who knew how long they'd been wrapped tight? I wanted to rub them, but my hands were tied solidly. I shook my head once, twice, and the rest of my bandages slid off. They lay in my lap, bloody, like the first page of Ulysses' poem.

I blinked a little blurriness away and slowly took in the room. It was narrow, but long. Waldo Fouks sat on an oil drum in the far corner, banging his shrunken feet against the side — *thump-thump-thump*. He seemed oblivious.

But he was my guard. I sat very still.

Humming to himself, Waldo toyed with a furry shape that squirmed between his hands. He couldn't see, but he sensed everything, weirdly, inhumanly. All at once, his hands flew furiously. The thing was trying to escape. Waldo's face tensed and his fingers tightened. A little cry came from his lap, and the thing with fur went still. Waldo opened his hands and the shape thudded to the floor.

The boy shrugged and wiped his palms on his pants.

It was a rat.

I thought of the bag of rats Ronny had brought home from his job at the middle school days before, when this insanity had started. Had it been only days?

Twisting my hands over and over, trying silently to loosen the ties, I focused my swollen eyes on the blank gray walls around me. Riveted wall seams, the smell of oil, the incessant grinding far below. It was a ship, all right.

Suddenly turning his dead eyes to me, Waldo

tensed. "You're breathing louder now than before. You got free from your mouth gag, didn't you?"

"Shut up," I said, hurting too much to mince words.

"Whoo-oo!" he sang. "Ulysses is a toughie! You wait." He started thumping his feet against the drum again, but didn't get up.

I bent one hand around to my back pocket, arched up, and dug into the pocket as quietly as I could. Why hadn't I used the knife when Cane was attacking me? Why had I forgotten I had it? Soldiers don't forget. That meant Derek was still with me.

I guess I liked that.

Using two fingers of my left hand like a pair of tongs, I dragged the knife from my pocket. That alone took a few minutes. When it finally reached the lip of my pocket, it slid and nearly dropped to the floor. I clamped my fingers painfully and saved it from falling. It was almost as hard to get the blade out, but I jacked it open. Gripping the handle as best I could, I slowly began to saw the rope on my right wrist. I'd seen it on TV a hundred times. It actually worked. The people at the museum had kept the old blade sharp. I only missed the rope three times, slashing myself lightly. I almost didn't even notice.

Five minutes, ten minutes, fifteen minutes later, the rope frayed and fell away. I was free.

Waldo's head jerked up. "You wouldn't be trying to escape now, would you?" He hopped down to the floor and turned on me with those dead eye sockets. "There's plenty of strength in these little arms."

I tried to rise quietly to my feet, but Waldo leaped at me with his bony hands extended. I leaned to one side and elbowed him in the neck. He went down in a heap, falling onto the rat. I shoved the oil drum on top of him. Waldo went still.

I froze and looked at his slack, open mouth. What had I done to him?

I turned away and slid out the door into a gray hallway, long and unlit, and forgot about Waldo Fouks.

Abby was on the boat somewhere. My father had said that the First had her. Or K had said it. Or whoever he was. Of course, he could have been lying. He'd tricked me into thinking he was trying to save me. He'd only wanted the book.

I made my way past three, four doors, trying to steady myself on the swaying floor. All at once, something came over me like a dark wave. This was what Ronny had felt in the cemetery, too. I knew it. It sucked away whatever life was in me — and there wasn't much — and replaced it with . . . nothing.

It was him. The First was on the ship.

A deep rumble of engines reverberated under my feet. We were moving. I smelled more chemicals. And something else . . . explosives.

How did I know what explosives smelled like? Maybe it was Ulysses who knew. But what was the difference?

At the end of the hall I saw an open hatch, and beyond it a set of iron stairs. Stepping through the hatch, I peered through a cracked door to my right. I could see that it was late afternoon already, maybe later. How long had I been out? And then I spotted them — what looked like rocket launchers set out on the lower deck of the ship. Firework launchers. I was on the fireworks dredger of Dicky Meade.

Suddenly, my mind connected the dots — some of the dots, anyway. Fireworks. Explosives. What if the hold was packed with explosives to blow the Wound wide open and begin the Grand Return?

Was that how it would happen?

Once the fireworks started, the end would come quickly and harshly. I had to be ready.

Was that right?

Some kind of instinct took over. I made my way up to the top deck of the cabin. It was almost funny how I moved like a snake now, low and fast. This body was thinner, leaner than ever. That, and it had the soul of a soldier, Ulysses Longtemps. What a team!

I needed to stop joking around and just move.

A cabin door appeared on my left. Somehow I knew that Abby was in there.

My senses were electric now. I pulled on the door. Locked. I placed both hands on the hatch handle and tried to turn it. Not an inch. I pulled out the knife.

Ulysses may have been pointing the way, but Derek knew Abby. This was both of us working as one. I finally understood what he'd meant.

Thus boy-I-was and man-I-am combined.

I was being both. Ulysses and Derek. One haunting the other.

I shoved the thick blade into the lock, then turned. The blade tip snapped off, and my hand shook. *Saber broken . . .*

But it had opened the lock.

With all my strength, I pushed open the door. It flung wide. I saw a lamp on top of a bare metal desk and, strangely, a giant fishless aquarium against one wall. Water sloshed over its edges whenever the boat rocked.

Abby was lying motionless on a flat table, bound, eyes wrapped in bandages just like mine had been. Her leg was cut.

"Abby, I'm here —" I started.

My chest was crushed by massive arms from behind. I cried out.

It was Cane.

I had walked into it. Abby was the bait.

My heart hammered in my ears, but over it I heard a squeak of wooden wheels on the iron floor. A wheelchair entered the cabin. The whole room filled with the smell of bitter chemicals.

The First.

The tiny form of a man sat in the chair. At least, I thought he was a man. Was this Dicky Meade? He must have been in his nineties. He was shrunken, a parody of a human, a bag of clothes with a barely fleshed skull wobbling on top. Wisps of tangled white hair cobwebbed his scalp. When he managed to lift his head, his skin sagged. It had the look of wax paper. You could read through it.

Not that you'd want to.

"Let her go," I said. Cane squeezed harder around my chest. I almost fainted. The thing in the chair said nothing.

He wheeled himself slowly over to the aquarium and muttered to Cane. One arm unwound from me but was back before I could move. There was a sound of gears grinding, and a harness — all straps and wires — came down from the ceiling over the chair.

Slipping his upper body into it, the First was

hoisted out of his chair, pulleys and electric winches squealing. His useless legs fluttered under him like rags.

It was disgusting.

Hanging in the sling, he was lowered into the water tank.

Minutes went by silently, except for the sounds of dead men on the deck below, setting up the fireworks. After being submerged in the tank for a while, the old man was hoisted up and settled back into the wheelchair, dripping all over the floor. The water ran off him quickly. It seemed to help him breathe, somehow.

The old thing turned his eyes to me. His left eye looked like a pool of filthy oil. His right one was a pale marble, false, a ball bearing that drifted around the socket, sometimes arcing up into his forehead when his face was down, sometimes scanning off to the side.

"It's time for this body to go," he said. I wasn't sure if he was speaking to me. "I needed it for tonight, but now I must have new blood."

"Let her go," I said, glancing over at Abby. It was lame, but I didn't want to play word games. "Let her go," I repeated in the same tone. I sounded either really determined, or totally crazy.

The First didn't speak at once. Good. I could use some extra time. Extra time for what, I wasn't sure. To try to understand what was happening.

"It's a long time, a hundred and forty-four years," he said finally. "Body after body turning worthless as husks. Through the years, I bled less and less. I had to drench myself to stay moving, until Dicky Meade. Old, senile coot! I finally entered him in 1982. That started my real work on the river." He paused for a minute, almost thoughtfully. "You take a little of each of them with you when you move on."

No kidding. I was the poster boy for that.

"Then, ten years ago, my dredging cracked open the vault of death. A tiny rip where the veil was weakest, worn through by hundreds of centuries to the barest gauze between life and death. Remember that, ten years ago?"

I remembered.

"A soul came through, on a mission. It traveled through the water that connects every inch of this earth, all the way down to that stinking bayou. I sensed that soul. I knew, someday, it would come for me. I met him once. On the other side."

Creepy as it all was, I knew who he was talking about.

"Ulysses," I said.

"Y-y-you," he whispered fiercely, his voice dripping with loathing. "That first opening in 1864 gave us hope. We could escape our torture in the afterlife. I did escape, but before my men could follow, you closed the rip."

"So why didn't you cut me in the bayou ten years ago?" I asked. "You were there. You knew then who I was supposed to be."

The First sat very still. "When I sensed who took over your body in the bayou," he said, "I remembered that there was . . . a book. I needed it. You had to grow up and find the book. And I had to be patient.

"After the train crash, you began to move. I knew it would come to you, where your book was, how to find it, what it meant. Ulysses was brilliant — *you* were brilliant. You saw the Wound and knew exactly how to close it. But the book is so much more to me."

All this time, Abby hadn't stirred. Now her head shifted. She coughed, then went still again.

Meade wheeled over to a steel bookcase behind the desk. There were rows of bottled chemicals lined up there. He opened one and sniffed it. The smell was overpowering.

"I bled, for a while," he mused, closing the bottle again. "What I would give to have that blood again. It doesn't belong to any of the bodies. It's not his blood, you know. Not Tom Bell's. It's mine."

"What?" My head spun.

"No, no," he said, almost in a whisper. "That blood came with me. The soul I was is *in* that blood. There's no more left. The book is the only place now."

What could he possibly mean?

"I don't have the book," I said.

"But where is the book?" he pressed. "You see, that's what I want to know. Where it is, so I can have it."

It struck like lightning. Had my father — K — stolen the book to keep it away from the First? Had he *not* tricked me?

"It's . . . it's lost," I said.

The First made a noise in his throat and began to paw his left ear, smoothing his few strands of hair over it. He did this again and again, like Fat Henry in the barn and Old Tom in the *Phantom*, two other bodies the First had translated into.

"Since I don't have the book — yet —" the old man began calmly, pulling a broken saber from a desk drawer.

I trembled. Was this Ulysses' saber? After so many years? So many deaths?

"You do it," he said, holding the saber out toward me.

"Do what?"

"The blade must be the same," he said, motioning

to Abby with the broken saber. "It's why I have stayed so long. You do it. I'll tell you how."

What?

This crazy old guy expected me to use the broken saber on Abby? He wanted to translate into her, and I was supposed to . . . ? I couldn't even think.

"I'll find the book," I said, barely able to speak. My chest ached. I tried to steady myself, but Cane's grip on me was iron.

The old man's voice was hollow, deep, and barely controlled, seething with anger.

"Too late now," he said. "You're a surgeon. You'll do it just right."

And then it hit me.

The blood. He wanted the blood from the book. It was his. Something — one of those chemicals? — - would draw his blood out of the paper, and he would . . . what? Take it in somehow? And he would live longer?

I looked around frantically for something to stall him a little more. Then, on the shelf behind his head, I saw the spine of a book I knew.

Afterlives by Tomas Deak.

So. The First had learned from it, too.

The more similar the manner of death, the better the fit. The less similar, the less the fit.

"Meade," I said. No one heard me, because at that moment, two men in scuba suits appeared in the doorway.

The First turned to them. "The stern hull is half a foot thick," he said. "You sure you have enough?"

The men nodded once and left.

"Meade —" I said again.

"It all starts now," the old man said, his mouth barely moving. The harness lifted him up. He leaned over Abby and removed her bandages, leaving her mouth stuffed with rags.

She blinked and saw me. Her eyes were frantic. She tried to scream. An awful, muffled sound.

Then I heard it: a low noise. Familiar. A voice deeper than human voices. It was the sound I'd first heard back in New Orleans the day Ronny had returned. The same voice I'd heard in the manufactory.

"Meade!" I said sharply, trying to stall for a few more minutes.

The old man turned his cadaverous face to me.

"K will come," I said. "He'll stop you. He . . . told me."

Meade's eyes rolled over me from side to side, like dead fingers stroking my cheek. He said nothing.

"Or my mother," I went on. "She'll find you —"

"Your mother!" he spat suddenly. "She paralyzed me! She broke my spine in the bayou. That's why I'm in this wheelchair!" He plunged the saber into his leg, and my stomach flipped. He sounded frantic now, frenzied. "You see? No blood left! Soon you'll be like me. You're the only other one who bled, you know."

"Why?" I demanded, my voice hoarse. "Why me?"

"We're charmed; we'll live long," he said, not answering. "But now I'm dry. I need my blood!"

I heard that familiar voice on the stairs below. With all my strength, I kicked back at Cane's knee. It was enough. The giant lurched to the side. I slipped from his grasp and rushed at Meade, knocking his skeletal hands away from Abby. He howled and slashed at me with the saber, cutting my arm. Blood rose along the gash. But nowhere near as much as there should have been.

Was I already changing?

Abby saw the cut. Her eyes flashed.

And then the voice I'd heard before reached the door. Hinges squealed as the door blew open. The lamp exploded. The room went dark.

⫷ SIXTEEN ⫸

The Hour of Magical Thinking

"Cut him!" the old man shouted in the dark. I heard him dangling loosely in his harness. "Forget the blood, just cut —"

"Derek, get down!" It was Ronny.

I ducked, and he swung a pipe. Cane yelled when it hit his thick flesh. Chairs crashed around me. Ronny struck again.

Splashing echoed inside the cabin, and a sharp odor surrounded me. Gasoline. My arm was wrenched toward the door by cold fingers. The room went yellow with flame. Cane's face was aglow.

Ronny freed Abby from the table. She swung her legs to the floor, but her wounded leg twisted. Ronny pulled her up in his arms and ran from the room. I was right behind.

Together, we tramped down the metal stairs and outside. Rain still battered the iron deck. I slipped but got up quickly. Three Legion soldiers rushed at us from behind the firework launchers. Ronny shoved

Abby over to me, then used the pipe in his hand like an ax. The soldiers dropped to their knees, and Ronny dragged us past the cabin toward the back of the boat.

Cane limped down the stairs, smoldering, following us. Abby jerked herself away from me. "I can . . . I can . . . walk."

"Try to run," said Ronny. "Here they come!" He pulled us to the railing and dived off the side of the boat, taking both of us with him.

We sank into the black river. I flailed until I reached the surface. I hated the water, but my arms wouldn't stop moving.

Gunshots pounded the waves. It was nearing evening and too dark to aim for anything. Abby's hand was tight on my arm as we let the current carry us downstream. Darkness and smoke covered us, and the shooting stopped. We made our way to the western bank and pulled ourselves up.

Torches lit Bloody Meadow. A skirmish was in full force in the woods to the north. The air filled with the sound of clashing blades, the pop-popping of muskets, and under it all, sinister voices.

"We're not done," Ronny said, scanning the field above us and wringing out his shirt. "As soon as the fireworks start, we're in even bigger trouble."

I thought back to the wreck of the *Eastport*, remembered the *Phantom* diving. . . .

"I have to go to the manufactory," I said. "Now. The *Phantom* —"

Ronny screwed up his face. "What do you think you're going to do there? Look, I don't know what kind of thing you have going with the ghosts, but we need more men —"

"Keep it down!" Abby whispered at us. She scrambled into the edge of the woods and fell to her knees, trying to catch her breath.

I knew time was running out. I pulled Ronny away so she couldn't hear. "I have to tell you something. . . ."

The way he looked at me, I could tell that he knew, right at that moment.

"I . . . died . . . in the bayou," I said quietly. "Ten years ago. Ulysses . . . he came into me. . . ."

He nodded, eyes down. "Your mother. She told you at Amaranthia?"

I think the patch on his cheek grew when I said yes. Tears welled in his eyes, but he didn't cry. He took it like a soldier told of the death of a friend. Like Ulysses when he saw Tom Bell die. Like me when I'd thought Ronny had died. Like Abby with her mother.

"Okay, then," he said. And that was it. He understood.

The meadow lit up with gunfire. Ronny called Abby and pulled me by the shirt to the southern end of Cross Crag. We weaved among the stones as a swarm of bullets pinged off the boulders all around us.

I couldn't believe the stupid reenactment was still going on. The confusing terrain kept different groups of men from knowing what was happening with the others. Already translations in the wet ground had swelled the Legion. There were hundreds more than those who'd come in the trucks. Their voices clanged in my ears.

Ronny peeked over the stones, but gunfire forced him back down. He punched his fist into his palm.

"What's the matter?" I said.

"What's n-not the matter? Look at it. We need to s-s-stop them. I t-told you. We need more men —"

"What men?" said Abby, turning to him. "There's only us."

"We have to stop the Grand Return!" Ronny snapped. "I c-can put stuff together. The explosives on that boat are going to rip a hole in the Wound so huge that there will be no way to close it. The Legion will push two thousand men into the water, the

Wound will open, and the Grand Return will happen."

"Ulysses stopped it with the submarine the first time," I said. "I'm sure he did."

"And what are you going to do?" Ronny sputtered. "T-take it into the r-river? You thought three hundred Legion soldiers was bad? Try thousands. After that, m-millions. That's how m-many will come if the Wound is blown open!"

Ronny was stomping back and forth down one of the alleys of the Crag. "We need men," he repeated. "Hundreds, at least. More."

"What am I supposed to do?" I said. "I can't make them magically appear."

"You c-c-can!" said Ronny. He grabbed me by the shoulders. His breath was horrible, rotten. "You can! Call them from the afterlife. You see their ghosts. Call up their souls!"

"Are you mental?" said Abby. "How can Derek do that?"

But I knew what Ronny meant.

After death, the soul resides exclusively in the afterlife — unless it returns in physical form. I knew what he meant, but the idea was horrifying. I couldn't force myself to connect the dots. "Ronny, that's crazy *and* impossible —"

"There's no other way!" he cried. "You saw what kind of beast the First is."

"But how can I?"

"You know how!" he yelled. "The ambush on the bridge. I heard the guide talking. You know about it. It was your troop. You were there when it happened! The souls could find their way there — if you call them."

Abby shook her head. "Ronny, calm down. You're talking crazy."

"Use the ambush," Ronny said, ignoring her and grabbing my shirt in his cold fist. "Use it to bring your troop back. They're loyal to you. They'll follow you anywhere! The ambush will happen again if you make it happen."

"What are you saying?" asked Abby.

Ronny let out a yell. "The souls of your old troop, Ulysses! They have to translate into the reenactors! There's no other way!" He was right up in my face. "Forget D-Derek. We need Ulysses n-n-now."

"No," I said. It was barely a whisper. "I can't do that!"

"You have to!" Ronny burst out. "You're their captain! You have a responsibility to everyone. Tell her!"

He flashed an angry look at Abby.

"What?" Abby demanded. "What is he talking about?"

"I . . . I . . ." I was frozen.

Ronny tore his hand away from my shirt. "I can't sit around and watch this happen. I'm going to try to lead the reenactors away from the river." He gave me a hard look. "You're Ulysses Longtemps. Be a hero again."

Then he was gone.

I stood in the rain, looking after him, and I knew deep inside that there was no other way.

"What was *that* all about?" Abby said. I just took her arm and pulled her with me through the rocks. The sounds of battle were all around us, but the fireworks hadn't started yet.

"We're going to the Long Bridge," I said.

"Derek, what did Ronny mean?" said Abby. "He was kidding when he called you Ulysses, right? Because of the poem?"

I didn't answer. Couldn't. I pushed through the outlying woods to the winding wagon path. A troop of reenactors saw us and called out. But by the time Abby tried to warn them, they had already hastened along a stone wall, away from the path. They didn't hear.

I marched faster in the drenching rain, breathing hard. The rain was its own sort of battle, pelting the road. It covered my face, washing the blood from my arm. The blood that made me special. The blood that was already drying up.

I paused in the center of Swamp Road. Abby looked around, trying to figure out which direction I was going in next. But I was already there. The Ghost Road. The road that led all the way to Ulysses' death.

"Come out," I said. "I'm here." I spoke too softly, almost in a whisper — like I had spoken at the bayou and everywhere else. Too softly.

"Come out!" Louder now.

"Derek," Abby said, "who are you talking to? Tell me I didn't really hear what I heard. Tell me, Derek."

I spun around to face her. This was it.

"Abby, I'm dead."

She stepped back. "No . . ."

"I'm dead," I repeated, rain dripping down my face.

"You're not," she said quietly. "Derek, please. It's scary enough —"

"It's what my mother told me at Amaranthia. I'm like Ronny. That's what this is all about. I'm the author of that poem. *I'm* the author. I wrote it in 1864. I'm Ulysses Perceval Longtemps. He translated into me in the bayou when I was four —"

She wasn't having any of it. "No! You only have to read the poem to find out what to do, but now that it's gone, you're getting scared. You're Derek Stone."

"Abby —"

"No! You shut up! Just shut up!" Her face was wild, dripping in the rain, her eyes on fire.

"Abby, I'm sorry. Ulysses came back ten years ago, because he needed to close the Wound. Now I have to call the others back to help me close it again. Ronny's right. We need them to help us win this war. Otherwise, we don't stand a chance."

She was frantic now, her hands clamped over her ears.

"It has to be done," I said. "I know what I'm doing."

"You don't!" she pleaded. "Even if Ulysses . . . *did* do that . . . Even if he did translate into you when you were small, it was a horrible thing, a terrible thing. He was a soldier. He had to do it. But not you! You're still Derek. I don't know Ulysses. I know Derek, and I wouldn't be here unless Derek is still here —"

"I *am* still here!" I shouted at her. "I am. But it's time for Ulysses to come out."

Musket shots pinged the stone wall to our left. I hurried down the road. I heard water splashing all around us.

"I have to hurry, before the fireworks start."

"Derek, please don't . . . ," Abby said.

But she stayed right next to me.

I kept on toward the Long Bridge. The road wound past the barn. I heard a voice, saw a shape in its murky shadows, but didn't let on to Abby. In my mind, I said one word.

Rope.

The shape saw me, somehow understood the word, then moved off into the darkness. It wasn't K. It wasn't Ronny. It was Madeline Donner.

I needed her help.

Maybe sensing her mother, Abby scanned the trees, saw nothing, and struggled to keep up with my wild marching, still arguing with me.

I stopped on the road and tried again. "You said you were ready. Well, now I'm here. I need you. I'll show you the way. Come out!"

This time they came.

◄| SEVENTEEN |►

On the Long Bridge

They came from the woods, from the sunken ground, from ditches, from hillocks, from behind stone walls. Four hundred came, splashing the flooded ground.

They were the troops who had fought with me in 1864, ghosts of the long dead. I knew they were good men. They wouldn't want to do what I was planning to ask, but they came when I called them.

Hundreds of ghosts massed in the road, every eye fixed on me. I knew them all. They were the men I'd lost at the Long Bridge during the Battle of Cemetery Bend. I recognized some of them from the barn earlier, only now I knew their names.

Every one.

"I need your souls to return," I announced.

A ripple of something went through the ghosts. Fear? Disgust?

Maybe.

But they didn't leave. I knew what I was asking of them. These ghosts were only the shadows of dead souls residing in the afterlife. I needed their souls to create a physical army to fight the Legion here and now. I was asking them to do what good souls had always refused to do — to translate.

"I need your souls to return," I said again.

This time, there was no movement among the ghosts, until Jem stepped out in front of them. He looked from face to face among the troops, and then at me.

"We'll do whatever you say, Captain."

My heart broke, knowing what I was asking.

Abby shivered beside me. "They're going to do it, aren't they?"

I nodded. "To the bridge!"

I turned and marched down the road. Four hundred ghosts followed me past the woods, the barn, the stone walls, to the site of their terrible death at the old stone bridge.

"Derek, don't," Abby said, stumbling along with me. "This is insane. It's wrong. Please . . ."

Her eyes were dark. She could have abandoned me, knowing who I was and what I planned to do. But just like the four hundred ghosts, she stayed.

By some amazing stroke of luck, the fireworks hadn't

started yet. The barge hadn't moved since we'd escaped it. As soon as it did, I would have to be down there, underwater in the *Phantom*. I hoped Ulysses' words would come to me then, but first I had to do this.

If I was losing my humanity, so be it. I was already dead. This had to be done, and there was no one else who could do it. That's what I told myself, anyway.

"Hurry!" I shouted over my shoulder, and the ghost troops sped up to match my stride.

Abby walked behind me silently. I wondered if she knew about her mother's role in all of this. She would soon.

We marched farther down the road among the trees, and there it was — the Long Bridge. Its seven stony arches leaped over the rushing water. I stopped.

The ghosts faded from the air as if they were no more than mist, and the water below the bridge began thrashing. It splashed and boiled with their waiting souls, willing to return if I needed them. I felt like some kind of creepy sorcerer, raising the dead in the dark, cold rain.

But what choice did I have? "Be ready!"

A minute passed. Two minutes.

"What's happening?" Abby asked me. All she could see was an empty bridge. "Are the ghosts gone?"

At that moment, Madeline Donner staggered out

of the woods, carrying the singed bell rope from the tower in her hands.

Abby gasped when she saw her mother. She wanted to go to her, but I held her back. She turned and saw no surprise on my face. "Derek, why is she here?"

"I told her to come."

Like Ronny, Madeline Donner knew that the only way to battle the Legion was with physical force. Ghosts couldn't do much against dead souls in bodies. They'd routed the Legion at Amaranthia, but that had only been temporary. We needed to stop the Legion here — for good — or there would be no stopping them anywhere.

"The rope!" I cried. Abby's mother strung it quickly across the bridge, pulled it taut, then loosened it with one end still in her hands.

I heard horses' hooves thundering through the woods.

Chains meant to bind, tore hooves asunder. We charged
Across the bridge. A few of us — no more — passed by
Before those chains pulled taut across the stone,
And sent both horse and man to ambush and to death
  below.
I hear their screams each hour since.

In my mind I saw the reenactors, acting like children riding to play war. They had no idea. But they were heading right for the Legion anyway. They were dead either way. At least now, my men would return in them to fight.

"I'm going," said Abby. She twisted from my grip and ran to her mother. Madeline's face was blank, but she lifted her frail hands to her daughter. It wouldn't last. The horses were coming. I knew what Abby's mother would do.

It would happen like this:

The cavalry bursts from the woods toward the bridge.

"Derek!" Abby cries. Her mother turns away, nearly lifeless, one last mission in her. Madeline Donner pulls the rope tight across the bridge.

Abby muffles a scream as the first riders shout, their horses' hooves catching the rope, which tangles the frightened beasts.

Six horses fall to the stones, beginning a horrifying chain collision. Pushed forward by the stampeding horses, the whole troop crashes off the sides of the bridge. Five riders, forty, two hundred hurtling into the water, to the souls waiting below.

That ambush on the bridge would be the same as it was in April 1864. I remembered it then. Except that what follows this time is the marching of boots, the thumping of hooves, the assembling of soldiers — four hundred dead good men to fight the Legion.

And I will lead them.

But that wasn't the way it happened.

My memory, that messed-up jumble, spit out one line of the poem again, and everything changed.

I hear their screams each hour since.

To a chorus of wild yells, the first horses galloped out of the woods, riders driving them as fast as they would go. But the eyes of the reenactors were filled with horror. This was no fake battle.

Was I really a killer, like the First? No better than that?

"No!" I shouted.

I jumped for Madeline Donner, pushed Abby away, and sent her mother running off the bridge. The rope fell slack to the ground.

The horses streamed across the bridge in one long line. Four hundred horses thundered past me and galloped off into the fog.

The Long Bridge massacre did not happen again.

I'd failed.

We didn't have those four hundred soldiers now. I couldn't kill innocent men. The Legion would have at least three times as many men soon, probably ten times.

We had only Ronny and Abby and me.

I watched the last of the horses ride away in the rain and wondered if the riders would survive the Legion. I hoped so. But hope dies quickly on the battlefield.

A minute later, the ghosts returned to the bridge. Jem stepped toward me, looking at me questioningly.

Something rose in me just then. Call it courage. Or honor. Or insanity. But looking into the faces of my troops, I felt we could *still* fight the dead. We could push them to the river and back into the Wound. It was possible. I'd seen it at Amaranthia. Me and a troop of ghosts.

"We can do this! If you have any love for the world you left, then take arms now. Push the Legion to the river!"

The ghosts' eyes — every one — were fixed on me. I knew I had them.

"You remember the first time we fought this battle, so you know that in a little while, I won't be here. The *Phantom* will take me away. But don't be afraid! Hope, if it exists, will lead us to victory!"

I was all flowery in spite of myself. I spoke like the poem now.

The ghosts made a sound that rumbled through my bones. They were ready.

Abby put her hand in mine and held tight.

"Are you ready?" I called. The sound from the ghosts grew louder. Abby's hand shook.

The ghosts gathered close. I could feel a spark of energy, like a storm brewing.

"Are you ready?"

The river below the bridge shrieked. Ghost horses, hundreds of them, galloped up from the water, streaming wet. My men were on them in an instant.

"Draw the Legion to the river!" I shouted. "Push them into the water!"

Their reply was a deafening roar of wind, cold and strong. Rain fell like sheets of iron and coiled around the mounted ghosts. The storm of ghosts shot away from the bridge and galloped through the woods, toppling trees with its force.

I watched them fly up to the crest of the field, then turned on my heels.

I hasten now. The end is coming near.

Without a second thought, I ran as fast as I could to the little black building on the shore.

◁ EIGHTEEN ▷

Lung of Iron

I slogged through the pine swamps, through the low growth and the mud. Abby was right behind me.

I tried to piece together a plan as I walked, but I felt like a ghost tethered to its haunting place. I kept going around and around the same point.

Explosives.

Only a huge explosion could cauterize the opening between the worlds. Ulysses' training as a surgeon taught me about closing wounds. Sealing the Wound — cauterizing it — was the opposite of enlarging the Wound. Both were violent actions, but they had opposite results.

One act saved our world. The other doomed it.

I had no explosives, but the First did. The hull of the dredger was filled with them. He'd use them to blast the Wound open even wider. I'd use them to seal it closed forever. Easy enough, right?

Sure. No problem. But how was I supposed to do that?

All I knew was that the poem ended with Ulysses in the *Phantom,* approaching the Wound. That was where it had all happened then, so that was where it would have to happen now.

The sky burst with light.

This was followed by a thunderous explosion that shook the air. The fireworks had begun. I had minutes. I ran faster, to the streets of Cemetery Bend and right to the shore. Abby stayed close behind me. She knew the worst and still followed me.

When I got near the manufactory, I could see that it was a smoldering shell pouring black smoke into the gray sky. Cane had done his job here.

Firefighters scrambled up and down the sides of the building with hoses and axes, but the damage was already done. I was surprised to see Professor Bloom stomping around in a rage. She hadn't gone back to New Orleans after all.

My bad ear ached suddenly. Waldo Fouks was lurking in the shadows; I could feel it. What would it take to stop the little creep?

"Derek, look!" said Abby. "The fireworks are coming faster now."

"I'm out of time," I said. "The *Phantom* is in the tank. Professor Bloom said you can get to it only from underneath. You'd better leave."

"Not a chance," she said. "We're doing this together."

Abby worked her way past me, slipping unseen down to the riverbank. Without a word, she dived into the water. I raced to the shore after her.

Waldo must have heard the splash. He stumbled out of hiding, from behind a garage, and shuffled unseeing toward the sound. Toward me.

Professor Bloom turned, on edge. "Who's over there?"

A spotlight whipped around from one of the police cars. Two officers hurried across the parking lot toward me, calling out.

I ran at Waldo, knocking him on his back like an overturned beetle. The policemen yelled, but I ignored them and leaped into the water. It was filthy, thick. I tried to keep my eyes open to see Abby, but couldn't. I hoped she had already found the tank.

I made my way along the shore, then dived deep and groped along the rocky ledge until I felt the smooth side of the metal tank. I knew it was sealed on top but open at the bottom, and it would have protected the submarine from the fire. I still heard Waldo squealing in my head. I dived farther, but the lower edge of the tank wasn't where I thought it would be. I kept reaching deeper and deeper into the water.

Finally, I felt the bottom edge, but I couldn't pull

myself down to slip beneath it and into the tank. My arms ached. My lungs screamed. I had no air left. Then a hand grabbed my wrist and pulled. Abby yanked me under the edge of the tank. I burst through the surface of the water, gasping for air.

"Thanks," I panted. "I was —"

"Save it," Abby said, cutting me off. She was angry. Fine. She might never understand, but she was there with me.

The *Phantom* floated half-submerged in the tank, its top hatch above the water. The air in the tank was hot from the fire.

Without talking, Abby and I raised the iron door on the front of the tank, leaving the way open to enter the river. I threw off the chains holding the *Phantom* in place, and we crawled up the side of the sub. One after the other, we dropped through the hatch.

"This isn't going to kill us, is it?" Abby asked when I lowered the hatch over us and shut it tight.

"You bet it will," I said.

No laugh? Fine. At least she was there.

I grabbed the crank running from the nose to the tail of the sub, and began turning it. The shaft turned the propeller, slowly at first. Abby joined in, and the *Phantom* moved quickly out of the tank and into the river, the hatch still above the water.

. . . playing boats and underboats along the riverbank . . .

The two of us turned the crank as quickly as we could, but I knew that the *Phantom* worked best with as many as six men, not a couple of kids. Never mind that. We had what we had.

I tried not to think about being buried alive, but that was what it felt like in there — an iron coffin. The concave walls didn't leave much elbow room but demanded a lot of elbow *grease* to keep the propeller moving. I dreaded the moment when we would have to submerge the sub entirely.

"We only have one chance to do this," I found myself saying. "Only one chance. One chance . . ."

Abby groaned. "Wait. How many chances?"

"What?"

"Derek!" she snapped. "I get it. But could you *not* be Ulysses for a second and just use the motor? This is not the easiest thing for two people to do, even if I am stronger than you."

I blinked. "Yeah, sorry. Sure. Use the motor."

She had already flipped the switch, and the rear of the sub began to hum. We moved more quickly through the water. The small porthole over the nose showed that we were in the body of the river now. In the sky above was a constant barrage of fireworks. It would be over soon.

We motored, half submerged, for another few minutes.

"We'd better go farther down," Abby said after a while. "You know . . . dive."

I nodded, pulled the lever, and heard the diving fins pivot outside the sub. Water slid all the way up the porthole, and we were under, moving a bit faster now. There was some kind of headlight powered by a set of pedals on the floor near my feet. As long as I kept pedaling, the light was just bright enough to illuminate what was outside the porthole. Even through the dark water, I could see the black hull of the barge in the distance. It had started to move down the western bank of the river, toward the bottom of Bloody Meadow.

I tried to focus. I had to do what Ulysses had done. I didn't have the poem anymore, but if I squeezed every last bit of memory, maybe I'd find the answer I needed. Maybe.

I crank the rotor shaft with all the strength of body I
    can muster,
Yet only strength of heart will see me through . . .

The sky whitened with bursting fireworks. Far below in the water, small lights — flashlights? — swung around the dredger's stern.

"We need to get over there," I said.

Abby studied the gauges on the wheel in front of

her. "Then we're off course," she said. "We have to go twelve thingies southwest."

"Degrees?" I said.

"Yeah, those."

We were quite a team.

Together, we turned the rudder wheel that many marks. The submarine shifted toward the dredger. There was movement under the stern again.

"What *is* that?" I muttered. Then I saw them: two scuba divers. They had attached something to the hull and were swimming back to a nearby motorboat.

"Abby," I said. She stared out the porthole with me. "When we were on the dredger, the First told the divers that the hull is thick there," I said.

"Is that a bomb?" she said, suddenly sounding panicked. "Did they just put a bomb on the bottom of the big boat?"

I shrugged, thinking out loud: "But if that's the explosive . . . it's so *small*. It won't do anything. . . ."

Abby shook her head. "Maybe it's just to sink the boat. The explosives are on the dredger, in the hold or something, right? What if they're just going to sink the boat because the big explosion will happen when it hits the river bottom?"

Of course she was right.

The rumble of the dredger's engines idled, then died. As we motored closer, we could see the murky bottom of the river below the black hull. Pieces shuttled into place in my head.

"The Wound . . . ," I said. "It must be below the dredger now. Right now." I pressed my face to the glass porthole and searched the dark water. I remembered lines from the poem.

Then all at once, I see a thing — I rush to write it down!

A ledge of stone like a giant's bone —

"There. Look!" I said. We drove the *Phantom* lower in the water, and the rocky ledge Ulysses had seen all those years ago came into view. It was a shelf about seventy-five feet long, narrow, but pure stone; it must have weighed hundreds of tons. It seemed like an outcropping of the guts of the earth itself.

"I can't believe it," Abby breathed.

The bedrock was torn apart where the dredging had opened it. Stress on the rocks had shifted the plates of stone under the riverbed.

My heart thundered in my chest. "Holy —"

The water rocked with an explosion. It was small, but tossed the sub backward and off our course. When the porthole cleared, we saw the dredger tilt suddenly. Water must have been rushing in through the hole made by the explosion.

A second explosion sounded, and the boat began to sink faster.

"They'll blow the Wound wide open!" said Abby, turning to me. Her eyes were wide, pleading. "We don't know what we're doing. Without the book, there's nothing we can do."

"We have to get closer," I said calmly.

"No, we have to get out of here!"

◄ NINETEEN ►

The Red Stain

It was all happening too fast. The dredger's stern sank deeper. Time was slipping away. And my brain wasn't working. I had no idea how to seal the Wound shut.

"Bring us closer," I said. It was all I could think to do.

"You're out of your mind!" Abby said, but she turned the rudder anyway.

What I saw as we got closer and closer terrified me.

It lay there under the massive ledge: a tear in the earth, as narrow as a sliver but thirty or forty feet long. It looked like fabric — a flimsy fabric separating the worlds — and it was torn, waving like ragged seaweed in the current. Seeing it like this so many years ago must have been the first time he really understood.

Grasping at the Wound to broaden it, to enter here,
Those hungry souls demanding to assault our world!

It stopped my heart. Who were those souls below us? Beauchamp's Butchers? The two thousand evil dead wanting to come back to our world?

"Derek!" Abby screamed, pointing at the dredger.

The big ship sank even more quickly, its bow lifting out of the water now. Its stern aimed for a point just north of the Rift itself. But I knew that that would change as it sank.

"Derek, it's going to blow if it hits anything. We need to get out!"

But my mind was back in the old *Phantom*.

I remembered everything.

Tom kept yelling that he had to make the Wound bigger. Ulysses tried to stop him. Tom fell on him with the saber. K leaped past Ulysses from behind and pushed Tom away. The saber jerked backward, and that all-important blood flew across the cabin and the book.

"I must seal that opening!" cry I. "Cauterize the
   wound!
I'll wrench the rudder quickly to the crux,
Collapse the hanging ledge upon itself —"

But there was a right place to collapse the hanging ledge upon itself, and a wrong place. The wrong place was where the dredger was heading. It would blast the Wound wide open.

"We have to slow down the ship's fall until we find the right spot," I said suddenly. "We need to ram the dredger!"

"Ram *what*?" Abby said, dropping her hands from the rudder levers. "Are you kidding? I'm turning us around."

"No!" I shouted. I took the rudder from her and steered the *Phantom* right at the sinking boat.

"Derek, we're going to die. . . ."

"I told you we would," I said.

"I thought you were kidding!"

I had hoped I was.

The dredger was pointed almost straight down now. We moved directly under the sinking barge. Suddenly, it thudded down behind our heads like another explosion. It nearly sliced the little submarine in two. The dredger's giant hull ground into our iron shell, buckling the plates and denting the tail — but not puncturing it. Not yet. The massive heft of it pushed us down toward the bottom. It was insane to think we could guide the dredger's massive weight to the right spot. I scoured the riverbed.

Confusion reigns as we approach the gaping Wound;
I steer and steer and steer and

That was how the poem ended. I had no memory after that. "Ulysses discovered exactly what would expand the Wound and what would close it," I said aloud. "But he had no time to write it down."

"Where did he crash it?" Abby asked, urging me. "Is that part of the code?"

The ceiling of the sub quaked as the dredger sank farther. My eyes burned. I needed air.

Then it came to me.

Maybe the poem wasn't a code at all. Maybe the real code was my memory, and Ulysses' poem was like a key. His words would unlock something in me that wasn't even written on his pages!

And of all the lines of the poem, one kept coming back to me:

I'll wrench the rudder quickly to the crux,
Collapse the hanging ledge upon itself —

And suddenly that was it.

Crux.

Ulysses — I — had used the word once before, at the beginning of the poem.

. . . playing boats and underboats along the riverbank
(His dubbed the Crux, *mine* Spectre *was) —*

Crux was the name of the constellation also called the Southern Cross, which only appears in the southern hemisphere. Ulysses knew that. I knew that. Of course, "Crux" meant "Cross," but here — *here* — Ulysses meant it to mean "southern."

I was supposed to look south, to the southernmost edge of the Wound.

I flung the motor in reverse. "Back the other way!"

"You're crazy!" Abby said. "We can't —"

The sub lurched backward, south, the weight of the barge on us.

There, tucked into the riverbed, was a shard of something encrusted with barnacles. Plant fronds waved slowly around it. The thing was unmoving and angular — a slab of old gray iron fused into the rock.

"The *Phantom*," I breathed. "I see it. The original *Phantom*! Abby, we found it! We need to steer there. Abby —"

She muttered something softly and slumped over in her seat.

Our air was gone. Our half hour was done.

I suddenly felt very light-headed.

But no. It couldn't end this way. Not when we were this close. I didn't know where the strength came from, but I locked the rudder in place, as I somehow knew Ulysses had done. Holding my breath, I hammered the hatch open with my bare hands. I had only seconds. Water flooded in. I pulled Abby's limp form with me, away from the enormous hull of the dredger, up through the water to the surface. We left the husk of the replica *Phantom* to push the sinking dredger on top of Ulysses' original.

I kicked as hard as I could and finally broke the surface, knowing then that Ulysses had never made it this far. The *Phantom* had exploded before he reached the surface, and all went black in his head. His body must have washed up later, his book in the cartridge box strapped to his corpse.

Lifting Abby's head above the water, I battled to the shore. She coughed and gasped; then her arms began to move. "Just a little farther . . . ," I huffed.

The air was suddenly filled with the cries of ghosts and the howling of the evil dead. The river thrashed at the foot of Bloody Meadow. It was my troop of untranslated ghosts, pushing the Legion into the water.

Plain old Derek could not have done all this.

But I was more than that now. The ghosts of my troop — a storm — had forced the Legion down the bank and into the river, just like at Amaranthia. Their ghost horses were pure energy, their swords like flames. Maybe that was all the ghosts could do — move things with force.

But it was enough.

My ghosts wouldn't back down. They battered the Legion like a force of nature, pushing them all right over the top of the sinking barge.

Abby and I had almost reached the shore when the river exploded.

The world exploded.

Giant columns of water burst into the air. The river convulsed from below, flying up and out, over and over, and crashing down like boulders upon the battlefield. Then a huge gulf appeared in the river. It was a crater that stretched from bank to bank, sucking water down into it like a vacuum. The wails of the Legion stabbed my ears, as they were drawn down under the surface. Wave after wave crashed. Abby was ripped from my arms, and we were thrown through the water.

My heart stopped, started, stopped again. I watched it all like it was a dream. The river turned white, then black. I was hurtled out of myself and back in and back out again. Miles came and went.

Years came and went.

And still I was moving away away away.

◀ TWENTY ▶

Brothers in Arms

The explosion threw me up and out of the water. I struck the bank hard and hit my head on a rock. Did I bleed? I couldn't tell. I didn't care. I knew that the blood would stop one day, anyway. It had stopped for the First.

The field was flooded. Everything was flooded. After the final blast, the water began to drain back into the river.

The world was quiet.

After a minute, I heard yelling. They were the voices of men. Only men.

Had the Legion been swallowed back through the Wound? I listened again. No shrieks or howls in my bad ear. Silence. Could it possibly be true?

I strained against the ground and climbed to my feet. *Abby?* I couldn't see her. I couldn't see much of anything. *Abby?* I thought I was calling out for her, but my mouth hadn't moved. My sneakers were gone, lost in the blast. My shirt was torn. I pushed my hair from my eyes and looked around the field.

"Abby?" I said, for real this time, but it was barely a whisper.

No answer.

I sloshed across the soggy ground. It was slow going without shoes. Sirens cut sharply through the air. I stumbled into a ditch, gagged on muddy water, and climbed to my feet again, taking longer this time.

"Abby!" My voice sounded like a little boy's voice.

She was nowhere in sight. I tried to unplug my ears. My bad ear was as dull as it had been before the crash.

Without the distracting howls, one clear thought rang in my head.

Find the First.

But there was no need to find him. He found me.

The woods burst with movement and he rushed at me, a nightmare of froth and rage. The white ghostly creature, boiling mad, galloped in on a wild horse. He was strapped into some kind of contraption made out of wicker and wood. Leather straps held him upright. His useless legs fluttered like fallen banners. Ulysses' saber waved in his skeletal hand.

I stumbled back. The horse's eyes were huge with fear as the First charged at me, hacking with the broken saber.

To translate into me? No, to cut me — any way he could.

My feet were stuck in the mud. I leaned away, fell to the ground, got up again. The mad horse wailed, and the First came at me again. I hustled toward the cover of the trees. It was so far. I heard the hooves behind me and dived into a flooded ditch, hoping the beast wouldn't trample me.

The horse twisted its legs in the mud and slid down to one knee. The First lurched forward, nearly out of his wicker saddle, within inches of me. I clawed my way out of the ditch and staggered into the trees.

There was a quick, small movement in the woods, and I was down again. My knee crunched on a fallen tree limb. This time, it was Waldo Fouks who'd knocked me down. He and the First had both gotten off the dredger before it had sunk.

Muttering, Waldo leaped onto my back, grasping at my neck, trying blindly to cut me. I tugged on the broken tree limb and swung it up out of the mud. It whacked Waldo on the shoulder. I sloughed him off and pressed deeper into the woods.

Where was Abby?

I ran along a path, but the First galloped up behind me. I fell again.

A shriek sounded behind me, and a cold hand gripped my arm. I turned.

It was Ronny. His face was a death mask. The patch of rot had spread to his nose and over his left eye.

The horse surprised him, rearing up. Its hooves clawed the air and knocked Ronny to the ground. He lay twisted and still in the water.

"Cut the boy!" the First yelled to Waldo. But Waldo hadn't caught up with us yet.

In a rage, I reached up and dragged the First off his horse. The whole saddle tumbled to the ground. The old man fell on me, a deadweight, arms flailing, saber slicing.

I pushed the broken blade away. He slashed at my leg. I fell back on my hands, crawled away, and staggered to my feet again. My eyes were flooded with swamp water. I grabbed a stone, pounded it at the old man wherever I could. He groaned, his gray head jutting backward. His neck was black.

He would die soon . . . or translate one more time.

Regaining his balance, the First swung the sword again, sliced my shirt, creased my stomach. There wasn't much blood — less each time I was cut.

"Ronny!" I cried, looking around frantically. "Ronny!"

"He's . . . dead," the First gargled.

I wouldn't believe it.

Sirens closed in. Fire trucks roared on the far side of the river. Voices wailed. Not ghost voices, not the Legion. Living people.

Maybe we had done enough. Maybe I should just let myself be cut, leave others to eliminate the dead who had survived the explosion.

Then Cane appeared, and I knew it was over. His dead face was half burned away from Ronny's attack on the barge.

Somehow Ronny stumbled to his feet then, eyes blazing, legs jerking like a puppet's. He wasn't dead, but he was close. His face was sliced open on one side. He fell on Cane from behind. They clawed at each other in the mud, each with the other's head in his arms.

One engine roared louder now.

The old hearse wove crazily through the trees. I could see Abby — Abby! — weeping behind the wheel. She drove straight at Waldo, thumping over the ditches, her face completely pale.

Waldo shrieked when he heard the hearse. He scrambled to get out of the way, but slipped and disappeared under the its wheels. A burst of black air coiled up from the mud.

The First gave a weak yell from the ground nearby, and the horse rushed at me again. It knocked me to the ground. The old man grabbed its neck and was dragged into the trees, heading away from the river.

He had escaped.

Abby bolted from the hearse. "Ronny!"

I looked behind me. Cane and Ronny lay nearly motionless in the mud. Ronny's neck was turned in an awful way. He wrenched his arms once, and Cane cried out, digging his feet into the mud over and over until he went still. A wisp of black smoke coiled up from the back of Cane's head.

"Ronny!" I sank into the mud next to him. "Ronny, what can I do? Don't leave me! I'll find you someone, a new body —"

"No," he said, his voice broken. "I was w-w-wrong to tell you to translate your t-troops. I should have known you c-couldn't do that. The ghosts pushed the Legion into the w-water anyway. I saw it. You sent the Legion back. They're gone. The Wound is c-closed."

I couldn't speak.

Ronny's neck was still twisted, but his features eased. "Maybe I'll f-find my —Virgil's — family now. I'll fight if I have to. But maybe since we defeated the Legion here, things will get better there. Because of you, Derek."

"Ulysses, you mean," I said, my tears dripping onto his face.

"I mean Derek," he said firmly. "And hey, sorry I wasn't your real brother. . . ."

I was going to tell him he was wrong when he twitched all over. His head sank back. A coil of dark air flew up past me and away. I held him tight in my arms, but he was already as still as stone.

"Derek," Abby whispered. "I'm so . . ."

I stayed there for a while, then pulled away. There was practically nothing left of Ronny but a cold shell. Anyway, he had been wrong. Over the last few days we'd become as tight as brothers ever could be.

I felt empty. Abby hooked her arm through mine and leaned against me.

We heard a wail of pain and something else — the clang of metal. Together, we staggered through the pine trees and saw Dicky Meade's body, a dead husk, as white and dry as sand on the wet ground. The slice mark on the side of his head was like paper peeling off a wall. He'd found a new victim.

"The First is out there," said Abby. "In someone new."

The victim hadn't wanted to go. I could see the proof of a short but fierce struggle. Nearby, nearly buried in the mud, was a sword handle. Abby pulled it from the ground.

The broken saber.

"He'll want that back," I said softly.

"Let him try to get it. It belongs to you, anyway." She handed it to me.

I stood among the trees, holding my old saber, and let the heavy rain rush over me like a waterfall.

Abby touched my arm and turned to the car. "We need to get out of here," she said. "New Orleans. My family is there — what's left of it. Grammy Nora. You have Uncle Carl. My mother's out there. Your mother. And your dad, whoever he is. We'll pick up the pieces."

I listened to the sirens coming closer. The First was still here, but maybe Ronny had been right. With their leader — the First — on our side, and after this defeat, the Legion would be weaker in the afterlife. Maybe armies of the translated dead were a thing of the past. Maybe there was hope for peace in the other world. And in ours.

Maybe.

It was nice to think so.

I know one thing: The Wound is sealed shut. My ears tell me that. The Legion is gone. As impossible as it seems, Ronny and Abby and I have done it.

My mother once told me, *"The Legion will fall, the Wound will be closed, and life can return. Not for you, but for the others."*

Maybe not for me, but I'm still here. Maybe I'll discover why I bleed like the First, maybe not, but for now I'm still moving.

Who am I?

I'm Derek Stone. I'm Ulysses Longtemps.

I'm Derek Longtemps Stone.

Sirens coiled over everything now. Helicopters thudded. We needed to be out of there before the police descended on the field. They'd mop up this horrifying mess. They'd try to explain it. But that was all it would be: a possible explanation.

If you followed this story, you'll know better.

I turned to Abby. "Let the hearse finally do its job."

She looked at me as if she hoped to find something particular in my face. I don't know if she found it. She just nodded and helped me put Ronny into the back of the big car. She slumped into the driver's seat.

I slid in next to her.

"To New Orleans," she said. "The long way."

I picked up the battered road map, cupped my dead ear, and listened. Nothing. Good.

Abby let her eyes settle on me for a moment, then looked ahead and shoved the old car into gear, and we were gone. Home.

TONY ABBOTT is the author of more than seventy books for young readers, including the bestselling The Secrets of Droon series and the novels *Kringle*, *Firegirl* (winner of the 2006 Golden Kite Fiction Award), and most recently *The Postcard*. The Haunting of Derek Stone is his third series for Scholastic. It combines Tony's fascination with the Southern Gothic tradition, a long-held pessimism about the future of our delicate world, and a basic love of spooky stories. He lives and writes in Connecticut with his wife, two daughters, and their corgi, Comet. Visit him online at **www.tonyabbottbooks.com**.